"We should have been paying attention to you," Piper conceded, obviously feeling guilty. "But, come on, Paige—we can't just forget the whole potion and incantation because of some conversation that never even took place. This house is evil. We have to cleanse it if we ever want it to be our home again. Otherwise, we'll have to move out for good."

"I know how you feel, because I was shocked myself," Paige insisted. "But whether or not I grew up with Grams, the message from her was clear: The house is a haven. It's not evil! She was so determined when she spoke. How could she *not* have been referring to what's going on right now?"

Phoebe glanced at Piper. "I have to admit, I never really thought it made sense, that the Manor would turn on us," she said quietly. "Paige could be on to something."

Piper sighed heavily. "Then what is it? What's going on with the house?"

Paige shook her head. "I wish I knew. But we don't have to move. We just have to get to the bottom of this."

Charmed®

Published by Simon & Schuster

HOUSE OF SHARDS

HOUSE OF SHARDS

An original novel by Micol Ostow

Based on the hit TV series created by

Constance M. Burge

SIMON SPOTLIGHT ENTERTAINMENT
New York   London   Toronto   Sydney

This book is a work of fiction. Any references to historical events, real people, or real locales are used fictitiously. Other names, characters, places, and incidents are the product of the author's imagination, and any resemblance to actual events or locales or persons, living or dead, is entirely coincidental.

S|S|E

SIMON SPOTLIGHT ENTERTAINMENT
An imprint of Simon & Schuster Children's Publishing Division
1230 Avenue of the Americas, New York, New York 10020
® and © 2006 Spelling Television Inc. A CBS Company. All Rights Reserved.
All rights reserved, including the right of reproduction in whole or in part in any form.
SIMON SPOTLIGHT ENTERTAINMENT and related logo are trademarks of Simon & Schuster, Inc.
Manufactured in the United States of America
First Edition 10 9 8 7 6 5 4 3 2 1
Library of Congress Control Number 2006925835
ISBN-13: 978-1-4169-2531-6
ISBN-10: 1-4169-2531-7

To Lisa C.—now and forever, the Termineditor

Many thanks to Terra Chalberg and Cara Bedick for recruiting me, and then cutting me endless deadline-related slack; to everyone in Simon & Schuster's managing editorial and production departments, who somehow made my schedule work; and a huge debt of gratitude to Liz L., who provided the framework for this story (and who has the CUTEST new baby I have seen south of the Mason-Dixon!).

Prologue

It was a typical morning at the Halliwell household.

If by "typical," Piper Halliwell thought to herself, *you mean completely and totally crazed.*

Like so many modern women, Piper had to balance her work—running the San Francisco nightspot P3—with home, as in raising her baby boy, Wyatt, with the help of Leo, her husband. If those had been her only two responsibilities, they would have been enough.

If, Piper mused wryly, watching as Wyatt frowned at a few stray pieces of cereal strewn across the tray of his high chair. But those two responsibilities were just the tip of the magical iceberg for Piper and her two sisters.

Piper, her younger sister Phoebe, and their half sister, Paige, were witches. And not just any witches. Their combined supernatural strength was known as the Power of Three, and when put to use—most often in the form of protecting

Innocents from evil—it was more forceful than almost any other brand of magic that they'd come across. The Halliwell sisters came from a long line of witchy women, and though their mother had bound their powers when they were young, an incantation read by up-for-anything Phoebe many years ago had given back the girls' mojo.

Thank goodness, Piper thought, reflecting on how often evil baddies came to wreak havoc on the sisters.

Wyatt gurgled at his mother and pounded a sippy cup against the tray of his high chair.

"Yes, okay, I hear ya," Piper muttered to herself. "More juice, coming right up."

Piper crossed the kitchen floor to the refrigerator and pulled out the white grape juice that Wyatt liked best. She turned, arm outstretched, ready to pour.

And stopped dead in her tracks.

There, sitting just in front of her, was a puppy. A slobbery, smelly, and *seriously* oversized puppy. The animal's floppy ears grazed the ceiling, and its paws were the size of car tires. Cute as it was, this was clearly no ordinary canine.

Under the best of circumstances, Piper was not exactly a dog person. She was *way* too much of a neat freak to have a real appreciation for furry, four-legged friends. A few of Wyatt's friends from Mommy and Me had dogs, and Wyatt liked to play with them, so occasionally she was exposed to man's best friend. But thus far, Piper had managed to keep her own home fur-free, demons notwithstanding.

Which begged the question of what, exactly, Cujo's slightly more cuddly cousin was doing standing in front of her breakfast table. Cute or not, there was definitely something strange, and therefore potentially demonic, about the animal.

"Leo!" Piper called, summoning her Whitelighter husband.

A glittery aura took shape in the middle of the kitchen, and then Leo appeared. He looked puzzled. "Something wrong?"

Piper jerked her head in the direction of the uninvited guest, who was now panting as it looked down at the couple. "Doggie demon," she said.

The dog opened its mouth and yawned, revealing enormous fangs, if not necessarily an overwhelming urge to make use of them. He lifted up a massive hind quarter to scratch behind an ear, nearly ripping the curtains from the kitchen window in the process.

Leo's brow wrinkled in confusion. "*That's* a demon?"

"Do you think I went out and adopted a puppy this morning? A freakishly oversized puppy that's drooling enough to wash away our entire first floor?" Piper retorted. "I'm thinking magic."

Leo nodded. "Right. Well, a demon dog is a

new one to me." As a Whitelighter, Leo had an in with the Elders, which meant that, oftentimes, he got the scoop on whatever baddies were new in town.

The dog barked once, almost playfully, before springing at Piper. Instinctively, she reached out her hands and zapped it, exploding the monster into the ether, but not before it took a swipe at her forearm.

As the clouds of dust, smoke, and demon debris cleared, Leo raced to Piper's side. "Are you hurt?"

Piper shrugged. "It's just a flesh wound." She held out her arm for her husband to see.

Leo lifted her arm in his own hands, waving one gently across the surface of the cut. As quickly as it had appeared, the cut healed itself under his Whitelighter touch. He smiled. "You're fine."

"I am," Piper agreed, sighing and pushing her long dark hair out of her eyes. She glanced warily at Wyatt, still gurgling away innocently in his chair. "No thanks to that one."

"You think Wyatt had something to do with the demon dog?" Leo asked.

"As a matter of fact, I'm pretty darn sure of it," Piper said. She strode to Wyatt's high chair and picked up his sippy cup. She held the cup out to Leo.

"Captain Bow-Wow," Leo mused, taking in the illustration of a cartoon dog that was printed across the side of the cup.

"Captain Bow-Wow, indeed," Piper said, shaking her head. It wasn't the first time that Wyatt had accidentally conjured up magic with his incredible reserve of powers. "Once again, our magical progeny has managed to create a monster all on his own. Should we be proud?" She rolled her eyes, more exhausted than anything else.

Working mothers have it easy, she thought. *Try working* and *wielding magic.*

"C'mon, Piper," Leo said, wrapping a comforting arm around her shoulders. He could see that she was upset. "I know taking care of a baby with powers is difficult. But look at it this way. Wyatt's okay. You're okay. I'm okay. No harm done. It wasn't the first time we've had to vanquish some unexpected evil—and I'm sure it won't be the last."

"*Almost* no harm done," Piper corrected Leo. She pointed to the corner of the kitchen, where an antique vase lay, smashed into various pieces, on the floor. "Thank goodness that vase will never again terrorize the free world." She sank into a chair, resting her elbows on the kitchen table. "This monster-bashing gig is going to boost our property taxes way up."

"Don't tell me we've got demon problems this early in the morning."

Paige padded into the kitchen, still in her pajamas and robe. Phoebe was just behind her, looking equally bleary-eyed.

"Really, I mean, demons who can't wait until we've had our coffee?" Phoebe muttered. "That's just . . . evil."

"Yeah, I think that's the point," Piper quipped. "But don't worry, it's gone."

"Do we even want to know what 'it' was?" Phoebe asked, arching an eyebrow and helping herself to a slice of toast that Piper had set out when she first woke up.

"A puppy," Piper said flatly. "It was a supersized puppy . . . with supersized fangs."

"Huh," Paige mused. "That's a new one. I mean, I thought we'd seen it all. Fairies, nymphs, Greek gods . . . but a puppy? Never thought there would be such a thing as a puppy demon. Demons aren't really supposed to be cuddly."

"Well, normally, I don't think they are," Leo said. "Piper thinks that Wyatt had something to do with it."

"And you don't?" Piper asked. She gestured toward the cup in his hands. "Exhibit A—Wyatt's sippy cup. It has a drawing of a puppy on it that looks almost exactly like the pooch I just vanquished. Exhibit B is . . . well, Wyatt's track record."

"And is the lamp Exhibit C?" Paige asked, pointing at the broken pottery and frowning.

"No, it was just in the wrong place at the wrong time," Piper said, sighing. "A casualty of our lifestyle."

"Occupational hazard," Paige said. "Things are always getting wrecked in the name of serving good magic. I mean, my dry cleaning bills alone are a fortune."

"It doesn't help that this house—beautiful as it may be—is sort of, um, falling apart," Phoebe said.

The house was a Victorian, a typical San Francisco style, and had been in the Halliwell family for several generations. Piper and Phoebe had moved in after their mother died, and Paige had joined them shortly after she was discovered by her sisters.

Phoebe ran her fingers through her short dark hair. "I mean, when the demons aren't taking us down, the plumbing is."

Paige shot Phoebe a sidelong glance that did not escape Piper's attention. She coughed meaningfully.

"What?" Piper drawled, her antennae up. "That was a suspicious cough." She raised an eyebrow. "Do you two ladies have something to tell me?"

"Well," Phoebe began, squirming in her seat, "we hate to be the bearers of bad news, but . . . the hot water is out."

"*What?*" Piper repeated, this time her voice a piercing shriek. She ran the faucet to the kitchen sink and plunged her hand into the stream of water. A look of consternation crossed her face. "Yeah, that's pretty cold." She turned off the tap and dried her hand on a dish towel. "Fabulous.

Of *course* I decided to put off my shower until after Wyatt was fed."

"Tell us about it," Paige said. "Neither of us has showered yet either."

"Great, so we'll all be stinky together. Whatever. Even if I had showered, I'd need to do it again, after that vanquish. The doggie demon had monster-strength slobber," Piper said. "Old plumbing, cracked plaster, and demons dropping in at every hour." She shrugged. "Do you think we can add a 'fighting evil' clause to our homeowner's policy?"

Phoebe smiled ruefully. "I wouldn't count on it, sis. Unfortunately."

"Well, if you girls can wait until the evening to take your showers, I can have a look at the pipes," Leo said. When he'd first been sent to the girls as their guardian Whitelighter, it had been in the guise of a handyman, which certainly came in . . . handy . . . in their rickety old house. "There'll be hot water before you know it."

Piper sighed for what felt like the millionth time that morning. "Is that a promise?"

Chapter 1

"Out of my way—I'm all about the hot water," Phoebe said, bursting through the front door. "I have been dreaming about this shower since I left for work this morning." She shuddered. "I'm telling you, my skin is crawling."

"*Eeew* . . . and yet, I second that motion," Paige said, hot on her half sister's heels. "You have exactly twenty minutes, Phoebe."

"Uh, well, I'm sorry to have to break it to you, girls, but a twenty-minute limit isn't going to do either of you any good when the pipes are still busted," Piper quipped, rising up from the living room couch to greet them.

"*What?*" Both sisters groaned in unison.

"I know, I know," Piper clucked. "I hate to have to say it, but we've made zero progress with the plumbing crisis. Leo went out for some new parts this afternoon, but he's still banging around down there." The distant crash of clanging pipes underscored Piper's news with impeccable timing.

Phoebe frowned. "A simple plumbing problem that Leo can't fix? Highly suspicious." After all, as a Whitelighter, Leo was a healer, through and through.

"I know, I had my own doubts," Piper agreed. "I did some close surveillance of the situation, but after a few hours of listening to clanging and four-letter words, I decided to leave it to the professional."

"Which . . . ," Paige prompted.

"Hasn't worked out all that well," Piper admitted. "Although his rate of shouting out four-letter words is slowing, at least a little bit. I'm taking that as a good sign."

"Well, that's a start," Phoebe said. She placed her hands on her hips in an all-business stance. "When was the last time you checked on him?"

"About half an hour ago, just before I put Wyatt down for his nap," Piper said.

"In that case, I think he's just about due for a another check-in."

"Really?" Piper asked, doubtful. "You think nagging him is going to do the trick? Keep in mind, we're trying to keep the colorful phrases to a minimum."

"Don't think of it as nagging," Phoebe suggested. "Think of it as . . . motivation."

"You two can motivate," Paige said. "I'm going to go change out of these boots. What was I thinking, buying heels like these? Why didn't anyone try to talk me into a more sensible purchase?"

"Do the words *I told you so* mean anything to you?" Piper asked. "But if we tried to dress for vanquishes we'd be in track pants 90 percent of the time. We deserve a little glamour—it's like a nod toward a normal life. The closest any of us is going to get, anyway."

"You're right. And besides, I think it's more of a 'too little, too late,' situation," Paige said, smiling. She pumped her fists. "May the force be with you—and the hot water, with *us*."

Phoebe and Piper clomped down the staircase and into the farther recesses of the basement, where they found Leo hunched over a cobweb-laced collection of pipes that rattled noisily. Nuts, bolts, screwdrivers, and other detritus lay scattered to either side of the handsome handyman. "This is weird," Phoebe said.

"What's weird? Plumbing problems?" Leo asked, pausing for a moment to wipe the back of his hand against his forehead. "Old house like this, plumbing problems aren't weird at all. I almost think it's weird that we don't have more of them."

"Oh, hey—" Piper protested, holding out her hand as if to block oncoming traffic. "No need to jinx us. Really."

"And anyway, it's not the plumbing problem that's weird," Phoebe said. "It's the fact that you're having so much trouble fixing it. Since when is a routine repair like this beyond you?"

Her tone was more flummoxed than accusatory.

"I guess, normally, it wouldn't be," Leo conceded. "But it doesn't matter—I think I've got it figured out."

"Don't tease, Leo," Phoebe said. ."If this means that I can shower, I will be your best friend forever."

"She really, really means it," Piper added.

"Well, then, I guess you'd better break out the friendship bracelets," Leo said, hitching his jeans up at the waist and rising. "I found the source of the leak." He pointed to the washing machine that stood in the opposite corner of the basement. "It was the washer. There was a backup in the pipes that was funneling all the hot water into the washer, instead of the places we need it. All this time, if we had been bathing in the washing machine, we'd have been fine."

"My hero," Piper said proudly.

"Mine, too," Phoebe added. "I call first shower!"

"Although," Piper said, looking pensive, "I would like to know where all the excess water from the washing machine's been going. I mean, you'd assume that the buildup would have to end up *somewhere*, right?"

"I'm guessing it just drained out the back of the machine," Leo replied.

Piper peered at him suspiciously. "Guessing?"

As if on cue, the cover of the washing machine flew up with a crash. A fountain of water spouted upward with the roar of whitewater rapids, drilling a hole through the ceiling above and showering the girls and Leo in runoff and debris.

"I'm guessing maybe not!" Piper called above the rushing waves. "This is no ordinary leak!"

"At least I'm getting my shower today," Phoebe joked, springing into action. She tensed her muscles and levitated smoothly, hovering just adjacent to the spray. With water streaming across her body, she murmured a quick incantation:

> *"Elemental powers, I summon to save,*
> *dry and remove the oncoming wave!"*

"Is it working?" she called, water rushing into her eyes and temporarily obscuring her vision. "Is it working?"

"I think so," Piper called. Her hands were wrapped around her head to protect herself from the force of the stream.

Reluctantly, Phoebe peeled one eye open to survey the damage. "It looks like the geyser is winding down at least. It's more of a level-one rapids system than a level-four."

"Okay, that's an improvement," Piper called, arms still folded over her head. "But I think we can do better." In a flash, she extended her hands toward the hole in the ceiling. A burst of light sparked from her fingertips and suddenly the hole was bigger. Chunks of plaster rained down into the open washing machine and plugged up the remaining trickle.

All at once, the room was quiet.

"Are we all okay?" Piper asked.

"We're good," Leo confirmed. "Thanks to your powers."

"Okay," Phoebe said, gasping from the magical exertion, "so here's a question. Which is worse: no hot water at all, or way too much water?"

Piper chuckled, taking in her sister's soggy countenance. "You know what, sweetie?" she asked. "I'll let you be the judge of that."

Chapter 2

A week—and several health club showers—later, the Halliwell plumbing system was fully functional once again. Which meant that for a brief while, at least, things could get back to normal.

Or whatever passes for "normal" around here, Paige thought. Supernatural occurrences seemed to be on the downshift again—no more over-sized animals lurking around the kitchen, any-way—and if there was one thing that the girls had learned from their experiences as the Charmed Ones, it was to enjoy the oh-so-brief breaks in demonic activity. Which Paige was fully prepared to do. It was Friday night, and after a long week of temp-work drudgery, all she wanted to do was curl up in bed with a few trashy tabloids. *Surely someone in Hollywood's got it worse off than we do*, she thought. *Someone must have shown up on the Fashion Police's hit list this week!*

She shimmied into a cozy pair of pajama bottoms

and pulled on a tank top. Her evening reading material lay scattered across her bed, and her pillows were plumped and ready for snuggling. Piper and Leo were downstairs watching a movie, and Phoebe was out on a date with her sometime boyfriend, Jason, who was in town for the weekend. The house was blissfully peaceful. She could not envision a more perfect evening.

But first, she had to wash her face.

With lots and lots of hot water, she thought to herself as she padded her way to the bathroom. *Functioning plumbing, how do I love thee? Let me count the ways.*

One—

Paige gasped as she turned the handle on the bathroom door. Where the bathtub, sink, and toilet had once stood, now there was only a big, black, gaping hole!

With a *whoosh,* Paige was sucked off her feet, pulled inward toward the abyss.

"Uh . . . Leo?" she called uncertainly. "Piper? Anyone? When did our bathroom become a black hole?" She braced herself against the door frame to keep from being sucked into the yawning chasm. "Just wondering."

The wind whipped against her, loosing her hair from its elastic tie and tossing it in and out of her eyes. She clutched at the door frame with every ounce of her upper body strength. Her toes scrabbled at the floor, trying to gain a purchase.

"*Leo!*" she called, louder this time. He had to

hear her. He was her Whitelighter; that was his job. Not to mention, he was only downstairs. The television wasn't *that* loud.

"Paige? What is it?" Piper called, making her way hurriedly up the stairs.

"Kinda hard to describe!" Paige called. "Get Leo!"

"I'm right here!" Leo called. "What—oh!"

"Yeah, 'oh' about covers it!" Paige shouted. "I think the first step is closing the door. Then maybe we can get to the Book of Shadows and find a spell or something. But I can't reach the door with one hand and don't want to let go of the doorjamb with the other!"

"Orb the open door to your hand," Leo suggested. "Then I'll orb you to me."

Paige nodded as best she could in the face of the tornado's force. She squinted in concentration, focusing all of her energy on the swinging door. "Door!" she called, waggling her fingers in the direction of the door's trajectory.

In a flash, the door swung toward her full force. It slammed into the doorjamb—Paige just managed to pull her fingers out of harm's way. At the same time, her entire body was yanked backward with as much force as the black hole had been exerting. Paige had a sudden and uncharacteristic flashback to her tenth-grade physics class: *For every action, there is an equal or opposite reaction.* With an unceremonious *thunk*, she found herself deposited in

Leo's arms. She looked up at him, baffled.

"Talk about space invaders," she said dryly.

Surprisingly, the Book of Shadows didn't contain any direct reference to strange portals into the unknown suddenly appearing in one's bathroom. The Book, a compendium of magical history and spells that had been passed down from one generation of Halliwell witches to the next, was more than a reference for the girls—it had practically served as a lifeline on more than one occasion. On this night, it offered a few spells on restoring altered states to their original forms, but little insight into what had happened to Paige in the bathroom.

"So, we've taken care of the immediate problem, but it's more like a Band-Aid than a full-time solution," Paige said, tapping her foot impatiently and surveying the attic. "And I have to say, I don't love the idea that the black hole can just reappear any time it wants."

"You bound it with strong magic," Leo pointed out. "I don't think it's going to come back anytime soon."

"But it can't be a bad idea to try and figure out what the problem was," Piper said, bouncing Wyatt on one knee as she thumbed through the Book with her free hand. He had remained blissfully unaware of the crisis, though his bedtime had passed several hours ago. "I mean, better safe than sorry."

"I completely agree," Leo said, "except that

you've been flipping through the book for an hour already and haven't come any closer to finding an answer. It's been a long week. I say we get some rest, and I'll take this up with the Elders first thing in the morning. Maybe they've got a line on what's going on." The Elders were a sort of magical high council, and as a Whitelighter, Leo had a direct connection to them—which often proved very helpful.

"If something's going haywire with the house, I don't think ignoring it is going to do the trick," Piper protested.

Leo rubbed her shoulder reassuringly. "No one is saying that we should ignore it. But the immediate problem's been taken care of, and I think we'll all feel better after a good night's sleep."

Paige yawned. "Maybe he's on to something," she said. "I've got some celebrity gossip and a cup of tea waiting for me. I say we make this priority number one—tomorrow morning."

"Fine," Piper conceded. "I'm not at my freshest right now, anyway. But I've got one suggestion for you, Paige," she said.

"What's that?" Paige asked brightly.

"Maybe you should wash your face in the downstairs bathroom. Just until we've gotten to the bottom of this," Piper suggested. She shrugged. "As a precaution?"

Paige nodded. "Good call, Sis," she said. "Good call."

• • •

Things did look better in the morning. The sisters may not have known exactly what was going on in their house, but at least everything seemed shiny and new. Leo was off, meeting with the Elders as promised, while Piper nursed a cup of coffee and spoon-fed Wyatt. Paige leafed through the newspaper, thinking that maybe deliberately taking her mind off of the wacky goings-on around the Manor would help her to get some perspective. Regardless, she was planning on spending the day going through the Book of Shadows with a fine-toothed comb. For as long as it took.

Black holes don't just appear out of thin air, she thought grimly. *Especially not in the home of the Charmed Ones.*

"No, they don't," Phoebe said, marching into the kitchen with her lips pursed in an equally grim expression. Her close-cropped hair was tousled in a serious case of bed head, and she looked exhausted.

"Since when did you add mind reading to your repertoire?" Paige accused.

"Are you kidding? I'm an empath. And the vibes you're sending out? They're so loud, I practically heard them upstairs," Phoebe replied. She kissed Wyatt's cheek and settled at the kitchen table. "You can't hide feelings like that from a chick like me." She smiled, then rubbed her eyes, looking slightly pained.

"You look like you didn't sleep a wink. Bad night . . . or good date?" Paige asked playfully.

Phoebe shook her head glumly. "Bad date. Well, good date—I'm always excited when Jason is in town—but, bad night. *Weird* night," she corrected herself. "Jason's great, the restaurant was great, dinner was great. . . ." Her eyes took on a faraway gaze. "He got a haircut and looked super-extra adorable."

Piper waved her arm forward in a "get on with it" motion. "All good news. And the weird part, Phoebes?"

"Well, I brought him back to the house, and we were . . . talking," she said, sheepish. "Then we went into the kitchen. And I had this . . . I don't know, this reaction. It was more than a vibe, but not quite a premonition. But it was like . . . like the food was crying out to me."

"The *food*?" Piper asked, her voice ringing with disbelief. "The food spoke to you?"

"I know, it sounds nuts, but it's got to have something to do with my empath powers," Phoebe said, rubbing her fingers against her temples. "Even now, the food in here—all the food that's ever been in here—is calling to me."

"What's it saying? 'Toast me, butter me, serve me at room temperature'?" Paige cracked.

Phoebe shot daggers at her half sister. "You don't get it, Paige. I mean, none of us are living the vegan lifestyle here. It's like the food has . . . died here, or been killed by us. And its life force, its essence, still exists. The food that's died here is in pain. And it's calling out to me. It's deafening."

She shook her head. "It's giving me a migraine."

"Whoa," Paige said, her eyes widening. "What can we do about this? Is there, like, some sort of exorcism that we can do on our fridge?"

"There has to be something," Phoebe said. "Because I definitely can't stand this much pain for too much longer—no one could."

"Did Jason notice?" Piper asked sympathetically. "I mean, not the food-talking part, but that something was bothering you?"

Phoebe nodded. "He could definitely tell that something was wrong. I didn't share my theory that the ghosts of Thanksgivings past had come back to haunt me. I just told him I had a headache." She winced at the memory. "I'm sure he didn't take it personally." She crossed her fingers underneath the table for good measure.

"Ooh, ouch," Paige agreed. "'Headaches' are definitely bad for the male ego. But at least he knows you. I mean, it's not like it's typical of you to come down with a 'headache' every time he's in town."

"Definitely not," Phoebe agreed. "And he could see by my face that it wasn't any kind of excuse." She squeezed her eyes shut tightly. "Trust me, for a thousand reasons, I wish last night had ended differently than it did."

"Well, that settles it. There's definitely something going on," Paige said, her voice taking on a determined edge. "And I think it's particular to the house. Thankfully, the temping is going to be slow this week. I'm only in the office Tuesday and Thursday. That gives me plenty of time to look into whatever's got our Manor on magical protest."

Paige had left her full-time job as a social worker a few years back so that she could devote herself more fully to studying her craft. These days, she took temp work as it came up so as to keep herself in contact with potential Innocents; and also to pay the bills. The nature of temporary placement meant that, if nothing else, she was rarely bored. And aside from that, her flexible schedule was well-suited to fighting evil.

"The house? You think the voices that I heard are somehow connected to the plumbing problems?" Phoebe asked. "I thought that we hadn't decided whether the hot water crisis was evil. I mean, it was crappy, and bad timing, to boot— but evil?"

Piper and Paige exchanged a look.

"That's right," Piper said to Phoebe. "You weren't here for the sudden tear in the time-space continuum. In the upstairs bathroom."

Paige shook her head ruefully. "And all I wanted to do was wash my face."

Phoebe bit her lip and looked inquisitive. "Share."

Paige sighed. "Oh, it was all a Charmed One space odyssey. I nearly got sucked into a black hole. It was a whole big thing. Very exciting. I narrowly escaped being whooshed off into the final frontier. We're still not sure what caused it, but when I tried to go into the bathroom last night, well—behold the great abyss."

Phoebe's mouth dropped open. "What did you do?"

"I orbed the door shut, Leo orbed me away from the door, and we all decided to sleep on it. We improvised an incantation to keep the atmosphere sealed until we could get to the bottom of the situation. Which we intend to do today. Hence, me being up before noon on a Sunday." Paige mock grimaced. "Didn't you get the note that we left on your bed? About not using the upstairs bathroom? Didn't it get your spider-senses going?"

"Yeah. No. I mean, yes, I saw the note, but I just assumed it was a repeat performance of the hot water problem." Phoebe folded her arms and leaned against the table top. "You've gotta be right. There has to be something going on here that we're missing. It's like the house is . . . turning on us or something. I mean, trouble always comes in threes, right? First the washing machine freaks out, and it takes Piper's and my combined powers to stop the flood—I mean, we're talking biblical levels of water. That's definitely not normal. Then you"—she pointed at Paige—"go all accidental cosmonaut. And now I'm being martyred for the sins of Julia Child."

"I like to think of myself more as Martha Stewart, minus the jail sentence," Piper interjected. She'd been a chef before deciding to pursue her lifelong dream of opening up a night-club, and the kitchen was inarguably her terrain. "But, yup, I'm sorry to say that you're right. Each of these incidents has supernatural written all over it—especially when you stack them all together. Leo's up consulting with the Elders now. Too bad he's leaving out the part where you're suddenly the Salad Whisperer."

"I can give him the gory details soon enough," Phoebe said. She looked queasy. "And speaking of gory, that veal that you pounded last week when you were making your famous scallopini?"

"Yes?" Piper asked warily. She had some idea of what was coming.

"It is not happy with us right now," Phoebe said. "I need a Tylenol." She sprang away from the table and headed toward the bathroom.

"Take the ones from the downstairs bathroom!" Piper called after her. "I picked up a whole new bottle at the market last week!"

Once Phoebe was gone, Paige turned to her sister. "She's right, you know," she said, her face drawn and her voice ominous.

"How do you mean?" Piper asked.

"About trouble always coming in threes," Paige explained.

"Ah, but you're forgetting something," Piper said, waggling her finger knowingly.

"What's that?" Paige asked.

Piper smiled. "Third time's the charm."

Chapter 3

That afternoon, Paige and Phoebe spent time in the attic, flipping through the Book of Shadows, searching for some clue as to why their house seemed to be turning on them. Meanwhile, Piper took Wyatt on a playdate. She had balked at first about keeping the date, thinking that it made more sense to stay with her sisters. But as Paige and Phoebe pointed out, the research was slow going, and it wasn't anything that they couldn't handle without her. Besides, each of them needed to maintain any semblance of "normal life" that they possibly could whenever the opportunity presented itself—and that included playdates. Paige promised they'd call Piper as soon as they had any information, and practically shoved her out the door.

Which, now that Piper was sipping a tall, cool glass of iced tea and watching as Wyatt and his little friend Ben pushed big plastic dump trucks across Ben's playroom rug, didn't seem like such a bad way to spend an afternoon.

Hear, hear, Piper thought to herself. *I'll drink to that.*

"Thanks so much for having us over," Piper said, smiling graciously at Liza, Ben's mother, and her and Wyatt's hostess for the afternoon.

"Oh, any time," Liza said, waving her hand as if to signify that it was no big deal. "Ben's dad almost always goes into the office on Sundays, and it gets pretty lonely. I love Benny and all, but sometimes you just need to have an adult conversation, you know?" She ran her fingers through her blonde bob and grinned. "You probably think I'm a terrible mother," she said, "talking like that."

"No, I totally get it," Piper said sympathetically. "Adult company is important. That's why I live with my two sisters *and* my husband." She paused thoughtfully. "Which . . . can be a whole lot of adult company." She leaned in conspiratorially. "Sometimes, it can even be a little bit too much. Three women, and one bathroom? It can get pretty 'survival of the fittest.' I'm sure you can imagine."

Liza nodded knowingly. "Which is when it's good to escape for a playdate, right?" She winked.

"You read my mind," Piper said, smiling and holding up her glass in an impromptu toast to the thrills of occasionally rejoining the world of nonwitchy, nonmagical people. Regular people. *Normal* people.

"Gosh, Wyatt really loves those trucks, doesn't he?" Liza mused, watching the boys as they raced their respective toys along the wall.

Piper shook her head in amazement. "He actually doesn't play with those kinds of things much at home. He's more into his bears, and tigers—you know, plush toys—and action-figure-type stuff. But, hey—change is good. If it keeps him entertained, I'm all for it."

"The dump trucks are Ben's favorites," Liza explained. "But he did just get this very cute plush police officer. His grandparents sent it—an apology for living too far away to be here for his birthday. Sometimes guilt can be a very powerful motivator."

Piper clucked in understanding as Liza crossed to a toy chest that rested against the wall. She bent forward and rummaged around in the chest for a moment or two, then reemerged with an oversized stuffed policeman. He was fully suited—minus any weapons—and looked rather officially adorable.

"That's definitely right up Wyatt's alley!" Piper exclaimed, cooing over the toy. "We've just gotten to the 'Who are the people in your neighborhood?' sort of books, and he loves a man in uniform."

Just like his mother, she thought, remembering Leo's mortal existence as a wartime medic. She adored pictures of Leo back in the day, suited up, and sometimes found herself nostalgic for the fact that she hadn't been around to see him back then.

Back when he was human.

"Piper?"

It was Liza, probably wondering where Piper had gone, off into the world in her own head.

Piper shook off the moment. She would never be able to turn back time, to travel back to when Leo had been young, and alive. But she had him now. He was her husband, her Whitelighter, her best friend, and her son's father. And that was more than enough.

"Sorry, Liza. I guess I sort of spaced out for a minute there." Piper shook her head. "I must need some more sugar." She held out her glass of iced tea, now nearly drained. The cubes clanked together at the bottom of the glass. "Would it be possible for me to get a refill?" she asked politely.

"Of course!" Liza chirped. "Don't even worry about it! I space out all the time—I think being a full-time mom does something to my brain waves." She took Piper's glass and made her way to the kitchen.

"I'll keep an eye on them," Piper assured Liza as she dashed off. She took the toy police officer over to where Wyatt was perched on the floor.

"Hey, little buddy. This is"—she looked at the toy badge sewn on the doll's jacket lapel—"Officer Friendly. He looks pretty friendly to me. What do you think?" She held Officer Friendly out to Wyatt, who took it with curiosity, poking and prodding the plush toy from all of its squishy angles. "You like that, huh?" Piper asked, smiling. "We could talk about getting you one of your own."

Suddenly, Ben shrieked as though the devil himself had appeared in the room. At the same time, Wyatt burst into high-pitched laughter.

"What happened?" Liza called from the kitchen. There was the sound of broken glass, which Piper had to assume was her iced tea refill. But what on Earth was Ben going on about?

Piper whirled around, and all at once, she had her answer.

Standing in the corner of the room was a police officer who had to be at least seven feet tall. Worse, the cop didn't look to be human; rather, his skin was the ragged and pilly texture of combed cotton. Warily, Piper let her eyes travel to the badge on his lapel, though she was fairly sure what she would find there. One glance, and her suspicions were confirmed. The neat, machine-perfect stitching was unmistakable: OFFICER FRIENDLY.

"Oh, great," Piper groaned.

"Piper, did something—"

FLASH!

On a dime, Piper turned, reached out, and froze Liza before she could cross the foyer and enter the playroom. No *way* would Piper be able to explain a life-sized stuffed policeman chilling out in this woman's house.

Wyatt clapped his little hands in delight.

"You're not helping," Piper grumbled.

She reached up again. Officer Friendly—who, Piper had noticed, wasn't looking all that friendly after all, now that he was fully animated—seemed to realize what she was up to. His red-felt mouth opened into an indignant *O*, and he raised his hands as if to ward off her powers.

"Sorry, buddy, but you're dealing with a Charmed One," Piper said, flicking her wrists and blowing him up. "I take no prisoners when it comes to protecting Innocents." With a *poof*, Officer Friendly was gone, and all that was left was a wisp of smoke.

All at once, Wyatt and Ben burst into hysterical tears. Piper figured they were probably crying for different reasons, but, either way, it had to be taken care of.

At the same time, Liza's freeze wore off, and she dashed into the playroom with no memory at all of having been frozen in time. "What happened?"

"Oh, they tried to stand up, knocked their heads together, and fell back down," Piper lied. "You know how it is with toddlers. Always trying to run off before they're ready. I don't know about Ben, but Wyatt can barely keep his balance for more than a few minutes at a time. But of course, that doesn't keep him from trying."

Liza paused for a stunned and suspicious beat. Then she blinked, and it seemed that the moment had passed. She scooped Ben up from the floor and embraced him. "He seems fine," she murmured, more to herself than to Piper. "You're fine, aren't you?" she asked Ben. Ben gurgled in agreement, all traces of Officer Friendly seemingly gone from his mind.

"Oh!" Liza said, as if just remembering something. She placed Ben gently back down on the carpet. "Your tea. I . . . broke your glass." She frowned, looking puzzled again, then shrugged. "I dropped it. Let me go clean up the mess, and then I can bring you your refill."

"Sounds great," Piper said, relieved that a broken drinking glass was, apparently, to be the worst fallout from Wyatt's latest little magical endeavor.

"You're . . . okay to watch them, right?" Liza asked, sounding slightly more doubtful this time.

"Definitely," Piper assured her, crossing her fingers swiftly behind her back as she spoke.

With one last glance at Ben—whose tears had all but dried, and who had resumed happily playing with his dump truck—Liza went back to the kitchen to fetch Piper her drink.

Wyatt slapped at the carpet, giggling with glee. He seemed to be over the untimely demise of Officer Friendly.

"Yeah, yeah," Piper muttered quietly so that

Liza wouldn't hear. "You got away with it—*this* time." She shook her finger at Wyatt. "Consider yourself lucky."

Although, she decided, upon further reflection, *"lucky" would be a day without a magical catastrophe!*

But why do I get the feeling that that isn't in the cards anytime soon?

"Are you getting *anywhere* with that scrying crystal?" Paige asked, sighing deeply and crossing her arms over her chest.

She and Phoebe had been camped out in the Manor attic for almost three hours, poring over the pages of the Book of Shadows. Paige had turned the pages incessantly, until she had paper cuts on every one of her fingertips, but she had yet to find an answer.

Since looking through the book wasn't necessarily a two-person job, Phoebe had perched in the window seat and unfolded a map of San Francisco in front of her. She was now holding a scrying crystal over the map, waving it listlessly, willing it to perk up and point the sisters in the direction of a brewing supernatural threat.

Unfortunately, she was having about as much luck as Paige was having with the Book of Shadows—which was to say, none at all. The crystal hung limply in her hand, pointing directly downward, with no force save for the basic scientific fact of gravity. She exhaled, and ran her fingers through her hair in frustration.

"Nothing. Nada. Zilch," she said, barely bothering to look up from the map. "This is driving me crazy."

Paige closed the Book of Shadows carefully, and turned to regard her half sister, hands on hips. "I guess it could be worse," she said, hitching up the waist of her jeans.

Phoebe arched an eyebrow. "Magic has come to town, and we don't know who, what, when, where, why, or how. It *could* be worse if we knew for certain that it was something horrible, and definitely out to get us. Beyond that? I'm not really seeing a silver lining."

"Okay, yes, not being able to get to the bottom of this is a problem, I'll give you that," Paige conceded. "But if you're not picking up any evil vibes with the scrying crystal, maybe it isn't a thing, or an 'it,' or a 'they' that's after us. Maybe it's just a sort of supernatural . . . hiccup."

Phoebe bit her lip. "A hiccup?" she asked doubtfully.

Paige shrugged. "Maybe that's not the right word for it. Maybe it's more like a ripple. A small force." She nodded suddenly, as if hit by a burst of inspiration. "A tremor?" she offered.

Phoebe's expression darkened. "You should know better than to mention tremors in the city of San Francisco," she admonished. "Tremors are almost as bad as black magic."

"Touché," Paige said. "I guess that's not

exactly what I'm getting at either. But the point is, maybe there's some sort of magic in the air that's affecting us, even if it's not exactly evil."

"A black hole in the bathroom isn't evil?" Phoebe asked. A black hole *anywhere* other than outer space seemed like a pretty not-good thing, in her opinion.

"It didn't suck me up," Paige pointed out.

"Not for lack of trying," Phoebe replied. "But I hear what you're saying, and even if I didn't, it's not like this crystal is doing me a whole lot of good. We're getting nowhere. And I haven't had a vision in days," she grumbled, referring to the premonitions that often helped her and her sisters to identify the evil that they faced. She hoisted herself from the window seat, dusted off her jeans, and set about refolding the map. "Time to try something new."

"What do you suggest?" Paige asked, yawning widely. She covered her mouth sheepishly. "Sorry," she said. "I didn't exactly sleep that well, after my little journey into the final frontier last night."

"Don't apologize," Phoebe said. "Whatever's going on, it's going to have us all losing sleep before long." A determined glint came into her eye. "New plan."

"Share," Paige said.

"I go down to the kitchen, make myself a cup of tea, and write a spell that will potentially reveal whatever forces are acting on this house—assuming that there *are* actually forces acting on this house." She nodded to herself as if affirming her own plan of attack.

"I like it," Paige offered. "Sound, strategic reasoning. I'll come with you; I can conjure up a potion that will maximize the spell's effects."

Phoebe shook her head. "Not yet," she said. "It makes more sense for me to write the spell first. Then, once you see it, you'll have a better idea of what potion ingredients will be the strongest."

"Good thinking," Paige said, her mouth stretching into another yawn. She covered her mouth and grinned. "Sorry!"

"What did I tell you about apologizing?" Phoebe said, pretending to be stern. "We're good. Or, I mean, we're good to go."

"So what do I do while you're writing?" Paige asked. "Other than brushing up on my potion ingredients, I guess."

"Take a nap," Phoebe suggested.

Paige opened her mouth to protest. A nap was just about the least proactive thing a Charmed One could do right about now.

But Phoebe cut in before she could say anything. "Don't argue. You snooze for an hour. You wake up. We solve the crisis—just in time to dazzle Piper and Leo when they come home."

"You could be on to something," Paige said, impressed. The truth was, a nap sounded extremely appealing. "Promise you don't need me right now?"

"I do solemnly swear. And I will wake you in an hour," Phoebe replied, holding her right hand up in a "scout's honor" pose.

"Forty-five minutes," Paige countered. "And you've got a deal."

The sisters shook on it, then headed down the stairs together.

I suppose there are worse things than being given some time to catch up on my beauty sleep, Paige thought, as she made her way down the second-floor hallway to her bedroom. After all, it wasn't as though she wasn't going to pull her own weight in getting down to the bottom of this supernatural scenario. Of the three sisters, she was the most adept at mixing potions; while Piper may have been Most Likely to Be Found in the Kitchen, it was Paige who'd spent the past few years honing her skills at witchcraft.

She paused just outside her bedroom door. The atmosphere in the bathroom had totally morphed back to normal the night before, after she and Piper created the binding spell to call off the space walk. But, as she'd told Piper, she hadn't exactly slept soundly. Regardless of how inured she'd become to magical goings-on, the incident had shaken her up. Having her own bathroom turn against her was definitely a head trip.

That's all taken care of, she reminded herself. *The bathroom is back to normal. And the bedroom*

*was fine to begin with. All systems are go. There is no
reason to be worried.*

She told herself this, but didn't quite believe
it. Still, she placed her hand on the doorknob to
her room.

And turned it.

And gasped.

"We're home," Piper called, walking through the
front door with Wyatt balanced on one hip.
"Where is everybody?"

She slammed the door behind her and
dumped her tote bag under the console that
stood in the front hallway. With a grunt, she
leaned forward and put Wyatt down. He smiled
and tottered off toward the kitchen.

"We're in here," Phoebe called, above the
sound of a running faucet. "How was the playdate?"

"Well, it was fun . . . ," Piper began, entering
the kitchen and helping herself to a glass of water.

"But not uneventful?" Phoebe guessed. She
ruffled her nephew's hair. "Hello, cuteness!" she
cooed.

"Not so much," Piper agreed. "This one"—
she gestured at Wyatt, who was gurgling away
obliviously—"decided to exercise his powers,
for a change."

"More plush puppies coming to life?" Phoebe
asked.

Piper shook her head. "Oh, no," she said. "This

one had an actual occupation—and a badge. Officer Friendly."

Phoebe smiled wryly. "And I'm guessing Mr. Officer was a lot less friendly once he'd been magically activated and brought to life?"

Piper shrugged. "Nothing a little freeze-and-blast couldn't fix." She sighed and tossed her long dark hair out of her eyes and over one shoulder. "The biggest casualty was a drinking glass. Tragically, it couldn't be healed."

"Even still, in that case, it could be worse," Phoebe pointed out brightly. "Though we have to cross our fingers that your mommy friends don't start getting suspicious."

"True," Paige chimed in somewhat quietly from her perch at the kitchen table. She'd changed from her jeans and halter top into a colorful tank top and lounge pants ensemble, obviously intended to optimize her napping experience. Unfortunately, she looked neither calm nor rested. "But, then again, why should any of us hold out hope of making it through a day like other, normal, non-Charmed people?" She rested her chin in her hand glumly.

"Did I miss something?" Piper asked.

"Well," Phoebe explained, "it's looking like Paige's room has become some sort of magical lighting rod. Or vortex. Or hot spot. Or something. Something supernatural."

"More space adventures?" Piper guessed.

"Mmmm . . . a little bit different," Paige said.

"And kind of hard to explain." She frowned. "You sort of have to see it to believe it."

"Can I have a look?" Piper asked.

"Be my guest," Paige said. "I think I'm going to avoid that room for a little while, at least until we get things more under control." She scooped Wyatt up into her lap. "I'll watch him while you check things out." She shuddered slightly. "It's not dangerous. Just freaky," she said. "See for yourself."

Piper pushed Paige's door open curiously, resisting the urge to squeeze her eyes shut. Given what had been going on lately—black holes, food empathy—she had no idea what she thought she'd find in Paige's room.

What she did find, however, was absolutely the last thing she would have expected. That much was sure.

As Piper stepped over the threshold of the bedroom doorway, the room took on an ethereal glow. The walls seemed to hum with quiet energy. Piper felt distanced, removed, as though she were watching the activity in the room unfold like footage from an old home movie.

Yet there was something off about the scene.

Once upon a time, Paige's room had belonged to Prue Halliwell, Piper and Phoebe's oldest sister. The three girls had grown up in Halliwell Manor with their mother and father. What they didn't know as young girls was that their mother, a powerful witch, had become involved with her own Whitelighter. After she gave birth to his child, a daughter, the girls' mother left her on the front steps of a local church, knowing that she would be rescued by the clergy and placed in an appropriate adoptive home. That daughter was Paige. And since growing up and meeting Paige, Piper and Phoebe both knew that, indeed, she had been raised by adoptive parents who loved her as their own—until they were tragically killed in a car accident.

Paige, Piper, and Phoebe were well aware of one another's histories. They'd gone over them time and again, determining bloodlines and magical powers, sorting out the past to strengthen their fight against evil.

Which made what Piper was now seeing all the more shocking.

The tableau before her was an image, almost like a video imprint, of herself and her sisters when they were young. The décor of the room had completely reverted to when they'd been children. There was Phoebe, dimpled and pig-tailed, sitting in a rocking chair in the far corner of the room, singing a lullaby to her favorite doll. Grams sat on the bed with her legs splayed out in front of her, reading from a picture book of fairy tales. Piper didn't have to get any closer to know that the fairy tale being read was *The Little Mermaid*—that had always been Prue's favorite. And just like always, Grams was flanked by Prue and Piper, who were mesmerized by the book in equal measure.

Seeing this all laid out before her was unexpected, certainly—why had Paige's bedroom suddenly become a portal to the past?—but none of these particular details were especially confusing. The scene could have been plucked from any rainy Saturday during Piper's early childhood. Except for one thing.

Sitting on the floor at the foot of the bed, happily playing with a dollhouse, was Paige.

Paige, whose existence had not even been known to Piper and Phoebe until a decade-plus later!

Someone—or some*thing*—was messing with the Halliwell history, and it was completely and totally bizarre. Piper now understood why Paige had been so freaked out. These were their childhood memories, unspooling like a home movie, sans projector—and the memories were *wrong*.

But they *felt* right, presented as they were. Which must have blown Paige's mind. Because that's what it was doing to Piper.

"I can't hear the story," young Paige called from her perch on the floor. She leaned forward and did some readjusting inside the dollhouse, then turned to regard her half sisters on the bed. "Can you please read louder?"

"Of course, sweetheart," Grams said, not even remotely surprised to find an extra charge at her feet. She turned the page and continued to read, this time projecting more clearly. She'd just gotten to the part where the mermaid pays a visit to the sea witch and bargains for her legs.

"She'd give up her voice just to find a prince?" young Prue chimed in derisively. She wrinkled her nose. "That's silly."

At that, Piper had to chuckle despite herself. Prue had always been independent. Though she'd had her fair share of experiences with love, she definitely relied on herself—and her sisters—first and foremost.

"She should be able to have legs, a tail, a voice—*and* a prince!" young Paige agreed enthusiastically.

Piper laughed again. Just like Prue, Paige was fiercely independent, and fiercely determined. She didn't see any reason why the sisters shouldn't have everything they wanted in life. That was why she worked so hard to balance family, magic, and personal time.

They would have really loved each other, Prue and Paige, Piper thought wistfully, a lump rising in her throat. There wasn't a day that went by that she didn't miss her sister Prue. How different would life have been if they'd all four grown up together?

I guess we'll never know, Piper thought.

"Have you *seen* the prince?" young Phoebe asked, waving a chubby finger toward the book. She grinned.

Yup, Phoebe was always boy crazy, Piper mused,

closing the door again and preparing to head back downstairs to real time.

At least some things never change.

Phoebe met Piper at the foot of the stairs, looking concerned. "Weird, right?" she asked.

"Um, yeah, just a little bit," Piper agreed. "No wonder Paige is so upset."

"Yeah. I mean, if seeing those images is blowing *our* minds, imagine what it's doing to Paige," Phoebe said. "Well, I don't have to imagine it, I guess. I can *feel* the confusion coming off of her. It's like her aura's gone Day-Glo."

"Okay, so something's up. First the bathroom, then the food, and now Paige's room. What do we do?" Piper asked.

"No word from Leo?" Phoebe asked.

Piper shook her head. "He's been Up There a while. That's gotta be a good sign."

"Unless it's a bad sign," Phoebe suggested.

"Well, aren't you just so 'glass half full.'" Piper quipped. She sighed. "You scried, and you went through the Book of Shadows, right?"

Phoebe nodded. "Check, and check. But I came up with nothing." She furrowed her brow for a moment, then looked at Piper. "Where do we keep the family photo albums?"

"I think they're in the console in the dining room," Piper said. "You want to flip through the pictures, compare them to the scene in Paige's bedroom?"

"It couldn't hurt," Phoebe said. "Maybe there's a detail we're missing, some message that we're just not getting."

"Good thinking," Piper replied. "Let me go grab them. I'll meet you back in the kitchen."

She walked quickly to the dining room, remembering the many battles against evil that she and her sisters had fought in the Manor. If the house's magic energy were turning against them, they could be in for a serious clash; the residual magical vibes that clung to its floorboards was sure to be powerful.

Piper reached into the cherrywood console where they kept the good china, silver, and other valuables. She hoisted out the photo albums from the bottom shelf. *This may take more than one trip,* she thought, scanning the tall pile of memories that generations of Halliwells had been storing in the house.

She slid her hands under the first pile—and then paused, gasping.

What was that?

She felt it again—a sharp, piercing stab that began in the small of her back and radiated its way around, deep into her abdomen. "Ooow!" she moaned loudly.

In a flash, her sisters were in the dining room, hovering around her with concern.

"What is it?" Paige asked, having snapped out of her funk upon hearing Piper cry out.

"I . . ." Piper stumbled against a dining chair.

"I'm not sure. I'm having these . . . pains."

"Can you describe the pains, sweetie?" Phoebe asked. "What kind of pain? A dull ache? A sharp stab? Help us out."

"It's . . . oooohhhh. Well, I'm not really sure how this could be happening," Piper admitted, clutching her stomach, "but . . . well, it feels like labor pains. It feels like it felt when I was giving birth to Wyatt."

"Uh, okay . . . but, how is that possible?" Paige asked. "Unless there's something you've been keeping from us. For, like, nine months."

Piper glared at her. "Obviously I'm not really in labor," she growled. "But . . ." She paused and looked around the room, then back at her sisters. "Well, this is the room where I gave birth to Wyatt. And, you know . . . that's what this feels like."

"So you're having phantom labor pains," Phoebe mused. "Why?"

"I've got no idea," Piper confessed. "But when you add this to everything else that has been going on around here lately, it seems like there's only one logical conclusion."

"The house," Phoebe said.

"Yeah," Piper agreed, her tone grim. "I think it's possessed."

Chapter 4

"Possessed?" Paige asked anxiously. "Isn't that kind of, um, hard core?"

"It's not good news," Piper said. "But let's look at the evidence. Forgetting Wyatt's recent bursts of magical self-expression—which are clearly totally separate—"

"And therefore misleading," Phoebe pointed out.

"Yes, misleading," Piper agreed. "So, putting those aside, all of the supernatural activity that we've had to deal with recently has been connected to the house. Specifically, it's taken the form of the house acting out against us. Which, in all the years that it's been in the family, it's never done before. This can't be random."

"I think you're on to something," Phoebe said, looking around the room. "So the question is, what could be possessing the house? An evil spirit? A demon? Has the house itself come to life?"

"With evil intent?" Paige wondered aloud.

"That seems so unlikely," Piper said. "I mean,

in all the time we've been here—and I'm talking not just us, but generations of Halliwells—the house has never acted out against us, unless there was another force working on it. Never."

She thought back to when Phoebe had uncovered a Woogie living in the basement, and when Phoebe's ex-husband, Cole, had cast a spell to access bad magic from within the Manor. Both of those incidents had been possible because the house rests on a portal to the underworld.

But that portal doesn't just open on its own, Piper thought. *The Manor has always been a haven for good magic.*

Out loud, she said, "And you've already searched the Book of Shadows?"

Paige nodded, hands on pajama-clad hips. "We searched, we scried . . . nada. Phoebe was working on writing a spell that might uncover what was going on in the bathroom."

"Yeah, but now we've got the bedroom and the dining room to worry about too," Piper pointed out.

"Not to mention the food in the kitchen, and the plumbing freak-out from the other day," Phoebe added. "Obviously, they're all connected."

"I'm thinking we're gonna need a bigger spell," Piper said dryly. "Phoebe, have you tried to get a premonition?" Though Phoebe wasn't able to cause a vision to occur at will, sometimes she could coax one out by touching an item that was magically charged.

Phoebe shook her head. "It's not happening."

Piper sighed. "Maybe we should consult the book again. Now that we've got a broader scope. Who knows—it couldn't hurt." She winced. "And besides, I need to get out of here before I have to remember my Lamaze breathing!" She picked Wyatt up from the floor and led her sisters back upstairs toward the attic.

The first clue that all was not well upstairs was the sound of a door repeatedly slamming itself closed and then open, as if by a strong wind.

"So . . . what do you think that noise is?" Paige asked, mock casually.

"Well," Piper said slowly, cocking her head to one side, trying to listen, "it does kind of remind me of the noise that the bathroom door made when it flew open from the force of the sucking black hole. . . ."

The sisters exchanged glances.

All at once, there was a loud, hollow, whistling sound. A gust of wind stronger than a hurricane sent the bathroom door flying open again, nearly knocking the sisters off their respective feet.

"Yeah, I'd say the black hole is back," Piper quipped. She had pressed herself against the wall to maintain her balance and was clutching Wyatt for dear life.

"We *have* to get to the attic, to the book. Can we break for it?" Phoebe asked, looking at her sisters.

Paige nodded. "For once, I'm not wearing a miniskirt, tight pants, or high heels. I can definitely run for it." She turned to Piper. "Are you okay with Wyatt?"

"Oh, I'm a pro at this. Besides, you're forgetting that if there's one thing my kid knows, it's how to fend for himself," Piper reminded Paige.

"Check," Phoebe said. "So that's our plan." She shouted to be heard over the roar of the wind. "On my count. One . . . two . . . three!"

She burst forward, almost levitating with the strength of her momentum. Paige followed closely behind, holding her arms up in front of her face to shield herself from the suction of the bathroom.

Just as Piper was skirting the bathroom herself, she felt the floor shift beneath her. She looked down to see the hallway runner rippling like a jellyfish.

"Heads up!" she called to her sisters. They hopped up and down like kids playing jump rope, avoiding the lumps and bumps in the rug—but just barely.

One last sprint and they were in the attic, and not a moment too soon. Piper slammed the door shut behind them, breathing heavily. She turned to her sisters.

"Talk about a house arrest."

• • •

"It's totally calm up here," Paige said, hands on her hips and willing her heart rate to return to normal. "Why do you think that is?"

Phoebe wiped her forehead with the back of her hand and gestured toward the Book of Shadows. "My guess? The Book is creating some kind of safe zone from whatever's going on in the rest of the house."

"So, we're okay up here, but we can't go out into the rest of the house until we figure things out?" Piper wondered aloud. "That's not exactly an ideal situation."

"We can always orb out if we need to," Paige reminded her. "I think we just have to steer clear of, well, the rest of the Manor."

Piper rolled her eyes. "There's no place like home." She gently placed Wyatt on the floor and went to stand in front of the Book. "I have no idea where to look," she muttered, flipping through the pages at random.

"I know. I mean, we pretty much scoured the entire Book while you and Wyatt were out," Phoebe said.

Piper stepped back from the Book and tilted her head skyward. "We could use a little help down here, you know," she called.

Occasionally, the sisters got a witchy hand from Grams or their mother when they were having trouble locating something in the Book of Shadows. Unfortunately, they didn't have a whole lot of control over when the magical assists came down.

"Anyone? Anyone?" she quipped. She lightly tapped the edge of the stand on which the Book rested as if it were a microphone. "Is this thing on?"

All at once, the pages of the Book began to ruffle, as if caught in a breeze. Pages fanned and flipped until the Book finally settled open on a spread.

"Thank you," Piper called, grinning. "Now, was that so hard?"

"What's it say?" Phoebe asked, scampering over. She jostled Piper aside and eagerly skimmed the open page. "Blah, blah . . . house, hearth, home, family . . . blah . . . watchful eye . . ."

"This is very enlightening, Phoebe," Paige said, coming to stand next to her sister and have her own look at the text. She wrinkled her nose as she read. "There—that may be something," she said, pointing to a passage at the bottom of the page. "Look: 'A house whose inhabitants turn against it will turn against its inhabitants.' The Manor has pretty much turned on us, wouldn't you say?"

"Yeah, I think we can all agree on that," Piper said. "But this is still pretty cryptic. Since when have *we* turned on the Manor?"

"We were kind of grouchy when the plumbing started acting up last month," Phoebe said. "But something tells me that's not really what's going on here."

"Hey," Paige said, as if a lightbulb had suddenly turned on above her head. "What if we're being too literal? What if it's not about us turning our backs on the house, but more about us . . . turning our backs on our destinies?"

"You mean, like being the Charmed Ones?" Phoebe asked, mulling the point over.

Paige nodded. "Think about it. Wyatt's been causing all of these magical mishaps lately, Piper, and I know that's had you sort of frustrated. And Phoebe—you've been dating Jason, which is great, 'cause he's not, you know, the source of all evil, the way that Cole was. But you have to hide things from him. Cole knew you were a witch. But it's not something that you can share with Jason. And I'm sure that gets to you."

"Of course it does," Phoebe murmured, obviously affected by Paige's perceptiveness.

"And me, well, I'm so overwhelmed by all of this Charmed One stuff that I quit my job so that I could concentrate on it. Which is a good thing—I mean, it's totally what I wanted to do. But that doesn't mean that I don't sometimes have regrets about leaving my past life behind. I do miss my job, and all of the people I was helping as a social worker. I love saving Innocents as a witch, but I do sometimes miss helping Innocents as a regular old *person*."

Piper and Phoebe were quiet for a moment as

they considered the truth of what Paige was saying. They took their responsibilities as Charmed Ones very seriously, and were fully committed to their destinies of saving Innocents. But Paige was right. They all struggled constantly to balance the normal and the supernatural. And sometimes, the pressure built up.

Had it built to the point where they'd subconsciously turned their backs on their beloved ancestry?

And if so, what could they do to turn their attitudes around? Had they been abandoned by their house—and their heritage—forever?

Before they could ponder the matter much further, they were showered in a rain of white light. It was Leo, orbing back to the house—finally.

"You've got great timing," Piper said, crossing to where he had materialized, hugging him, and kissing him quickly on the lips. She filled him in. "The Manor's gone crazy."

Leo nodded. "I heard. *They* heard. That's what we were talking about."

Phoebe leveled a serious expression at him. "So . . . the fact that you were Up There for the entire afternoon is a good thing, or a very, very bad thing?"

Leo smiled. "Actually, a little bit of both. There's no question that the house is acting out against you."

Piper arched an eyebrow. "You don't say?"

"That much we figured out ourselves," Paige mentioned. "Not that we don't appreciate others' insights." She folded her arms across her chest.

"Well, as Piper pointed out, the house has never just up and turned on its inhabitants without being influenced by an outside force," Leo continued. "That having been said, given the number of battles that have been waged here—given how many different demons and other creatures that have manifested here—there's an infinite amount of magical energy coursing through the house's foundation. For better or for worse. And some of that residual magic could be what's working against you right now."

"But what about this passage?" Paige said, pointing toward the Book of Shadows excerpt the girls had just been reading. "About us turning against the house? Do you think our ambivalence about our calling could be what's causing the haunted-house routine?"

"It definitely could be," Leo agreed. "And there's really only one thing to do about it."

"Which is?" Piper prompted her husband.

"We have to cleanse the house of the . . . well, I guess, 'bad vibes' is the best term that I can come up with. We'll have to cast a spell on the house that, first, exorcises any bad vibes, and then restores the Manor to a haven of stability and love. There should be a passage in the Book about the sort of spell that will do the trick."

"Spells we can do. Spells are not a problem," Phoebe, their resident spell expert, said. "This could be worse. The sooner we get on this whole exorcism thing, the sooner we have our home, sweet home back."

"Actually," Leo hedged, looking uncomfortable, "it is worse. A little bit worse, that is."

"Worse, like how?" Piper asked, shaking her head. "Is there some sort of ritual sacrifice involved in the cleansing?"

"Not quite," Leo said. "But the process . . . well, it takes a while."

"Define 'a while,'" Phoebe said, looking at Leo nervously.

"It takes six months," Leo finally said. "The process takes six months from the time that you say the spell and perform the exorcism."

"So we have to deal with six more months of our house freaking out on us?" Paige asked, incredulous.

"More like, you have to deal with six months of being displaced," Leo clarified. "We're going to have to find a short-term rental, and move out. If any family enters the house during the six-month cleansing process, the spell will be broken. *And* we'd have to start all over again— or go on dealing with psychotic plumbing and impromptu black holes."

"So we have to pack up and move out, like, this week?" Phoebe asked in disbelief.

"Well, from what I know of, the cleansing

potions will take forty-eight hours to brew, at which point you can say the spell. And *then* we'll move out."

"That stinks," Paige said, her voice taking on a high-pitched, plaintive tone. "How are we going to do all of this in just two days?"

Chapter 5

"Thanks for meeting me in the middle of the afternoon," Phoebe said to Piper as her sister pulled smoothly into a curbside parking space. "I called all over town. This New Age shop is the only place that sells dried lavender this time of year. And lavender is the number one ingredient for the house-cleansing potion. So we couldn't exactly substitute." She laughed. "Thank goodness we live in San Francisco, right?"

"Totally, and it's not a problem, coming out here," Piper said, killing the ignition, stepping out of the car, and locking it in one swift motion. "Paige was happy to watch over Wyatt for a few hours."

"I talked to Elyse," Phoebe said, referring to her boss at the *Bay Mirror*, where Phoebe worked as an advice columnist. "She's okay with me working half days today and tomorrow so I can help prep for the move. Besides, I can always work on some letters from home. I just have to stop by the office after our errand to pick up some backed-up mail. Those piles can get seriously out of control."

"I believe it. What'd you end up telling Elyse about why we have to relocate?" Piper asked, all too familiar with the elaborate subterfuge that tended to go hand in hand with being a witch.

Phoebe shrugged. "Termites. Deep foundation rot."

"Not bad," Piper said, impressed. "It *is* sort of like that—if termites were magical little buggers. Here," she said, digging in her purse as they made their way into the holistic medicine shop where they frequently bought ingredients for spell casting. "I have a whole list for us. But, like you said, the dried lavender is crucial. It keeps longer and works more consistently than fresh herbs do."

"I'm not all that worried about the reasoning, as long as it does the trick," Phoebe said, holding the door open for Piper. Wind chimes tinkled as the door closed behind them, and multicolored light bounced from the faceted surfaces of various hanging sun catchers.

Phoebe glanced at the list Piper had drawn up. "You take the lavender and thyme. Those are for the cleansing. I'll get the honey and the rose petals. Rose is supposed to restore love to the house." The store was well stocked and well organized; all of the perishables were located on shelves toward the back, while brightly colored crystals, totems, and charms lined the prime real estate of the windows and the front tables.

"Honey we have at home," Piper said. She allowed herself a small smile. "I love it when the ingredients aren't too esoteric."

"Yeah, once in a while the elements cut us a break." Phoebe grinned as well, and began to pore over the shelves.

It was hard to focus, being surrounded by so many interesting and potent objects, but both girls knew that time was of the essence. Two days was barely enough time to pack up their belongings and say good-bye—albeit temporarily—to their home.

The sisters had nearly gathered all of the ingredients when a shop worker emerged from the back room. She was dressed in San Francisco haute crunch, from her wild, flowing blonde curls to her makeup-free face, right down past her floral tank dress to the tips of her sandaled feet. She was obviously very much at home in the shop.

"Are you finding everything okay?" she asked, smiling warmly.

Piper nodded. "Actually, your timing's perfect. I think we're all set," she said. She and Phoebe made their way up to the counter and laid out their purchases.

The clerk scanned each item through the register. "Trying to repurify a house?" she guessed.

"Is it that obvious?" Piper asked ruefully.

"Let's just say I know my way around this shop," the clerk said kindly. "You've got all the right tools for it, you know. So you're on the right track. In addition to the rose petals, it's helpful to balance rose quartzes in the far points of the area you're trying to cleanse. The stones channel the energy so that it gets evenly distributed and absorbed. Shall I get you a few of those?"

Piper and Phoebe exchanged a glance.

"That would be a great idea," Phoebe said. "I don't suppose they come in bulk?"

Rose quartz added to their bounty, Phoebe and Piper paid for their ingredients, thanked the shopkeeper again, and headed back to their car.

"When I get home, I'll get started on the potion," Piper said. "It should be ready by the time you get in tonight."

"Sounds good," Phoebe said. "I don't think I'll be at the office that long. We can work on the incantation before dinner."

"Which, now that you mention it, should be around seven," Piper said. "Leo's out house hunting this afternoon, and he found a few places that we can have furnished, short-term, for the right price. I think he wanted to show us the floor plans and photos of the top choices. He talked to Darryl, and they're all in decent neighborhoods." Darryl was a friend of the sisters who also happened to be a police officer. It came in handy, having someone in law enforcement who could help them handle supernatural evil—since problems with demons, et cetera, weren't exactly something they could take to the local police on a regular basis.

"I can't believe Leo's got some potential places for us already," Phoebe said, reaching into her bag and fishing out a pair of aviator shades. She slipped them on to protect her eyes from the strong midafternoon sun. "I guess I was secretly hoping that it would take longer."

"Me, too," Piper admitted, glancing down at the sidewalk. "I was sort of holding out for something to go wrong with the rental and some other option to present itself. But I was just kidding myself, obviously."

"We all were, sweetie," Phoebe said, wrapping an arm around Piper's shoulders and squeezing her sister tightly. "Paige was right. We've all questioned our identities as witches on lots of occasions. How could we help it? It's a huge legacy to live up to. But I had no idea we were, in effect, turning our backs on our house."

"Our *home*," Piper corrected. "And I know exactly what you mean. I guess I take for granted that the Manor has always been there for us. Even before we knew we were witches. But when I think about the things that have happened to us in that house . . ." Her voice trailed off as she became lost in thought.

"Your wedding," Phoebe said, remembering the day fondly. "And the first time you met Leo."

"It was the first time that *you* met Leo too!" Piper reminded her. "And let's just say that neither of us were exactly impervious to his, uh, charms." She grinned again, thinking back to the thunderbolt she'd felt upon first laying eyes on her Whitelighter, the man who would become her husband. He was adorable—which Phoebe had noticed too!

"Yeah," Phoebe said, blushing slightly at the memory. "Talk about barking up the wrong tree. Right from the start, he only had eyes for you."

"Do you remember when you agreed to move back home?" Piper asked gently.

Phoebe nodded. "After Grams died. You and Prue called me back to California. I was going through my rebellious phase in New York. I thought I was going to come in for the funeral, pay my respects, and get the heck out of Dodge. Things were so tense with Prue and me."

"And I was *so* sick of being a mediator," Piper added. "But it was nice to have you home, to have us back together again. I remember that."

"And then I found the Book of Shadows, and I read from it," Phoebe said. "And then everything changed."

The two girls were silent for a moment, memories flooding their minds.

"It's going to be hard, moving out of the Manor for six whole months," Piper said finally. "Would I sound totally bratty if I told you I didn't want to do it?"

Phoebe shook her head emphatically. "No brattier than me!" she insisted. "I hate the thought of moving too. But, you know, maybe it took something drastic like this to make us appreciate how important the Manor is to us. It's more than a home, it's a touchstone."

"You're right," Piper said. "And we have to do whatever it takes to cleanse it and keep it safe for us, and for all Halliwells, forever."

"Definitely," Phoebe agreed. "You go home and get to work on the potion. I'll swing by the office, and then tonight, we'll get the incantation written. Our house will be a home again—if the Power of Three has anything to say about it!"

At that, Piper had to laugh out loud. "Hear, hear," she said. "Hear, hear."

As the sisters wandered down the street and back toward their cars, Piper was surprised to hear her name being called.

"I thought that was you!"

Piper looked up to find a frazzled redhead standing in front of her and Phoebe. "Oh, hi, Emma," she said, recognizing the woman from Mommy and Me. She self-consciously adjusted the packages under her arm. Emma was the biggest gossip in the group, Piper knew. The last thing she needed was for all of the Mommies to know that she was practicing witchcraft in her spare time! "This is my sister Phoebe," she said, nodding her head in Phoebe's direction by way of introduction. "We were just doing some . . ."

"Shopping!" Phoebe finished brightly. "We love to shop!"

"I recognized you from the photo in your column," Emma said to Phoebe, smiling. "You're even prettier in person."

Phoebe blushed. "Thanks!" she replied.

"Were you two coming out of . . . *that* shop?" Emma continued cautiously, pointing a finger at the New Age store that they had, of course, just come out of.

"W-well, um," Piper stammered, not sure how to go about responding, "we've been having some work done on the house, like I mentioned. . . ." She paused, not knowing where to take her story.

"So we were in that shop," Phoebe jumped in, "because our other sister, Paige, is really into feng shui. So she wanted us to pick up some crystal paperweights for the new room, for when we're finished. She's a little"—Phoebe rolled her eyes affectionately—"goofy, you know. But what could it hurt?"

"Exactly, what could it hurt?" Piper chimed in, giving her best hearty laugh.

"Well, I suppose you're right!" Emma agreed, looking amused, if not completely without suspicion. "Well, I should get going. I have to pick up Russ from day care in a half an hour. But I'll see you at the next Mommy and Me, Piper." To Phoebe she said, "Great to meet you.

And good luck with the renovations on your—"

"Dining room!" Phoebe said.

"Kitchen!" Piper called out, at exactly the same moment.

"We're . . . getting our dining room *and* kitchen remodeled," Piper said weakly, trying to ignore the confused look on Emma's face.

"Right," Emma said, sounding dubious. "Well, good luck with that!"

Okay, well, at least I'm not the only one who has a serious attachment to my childhood home, Phoebe said to herself.

The thought brought her little comfort. It had been about an hour since she'd left Piper and headed back to her office downtown, and sifting through the letters from her readers had only served to drag her mood down further.

There must be something in the air this week, she decided. Nearly every other letter was from someone who had problems involving his or her childhood home. She had planned on running in, grabbing a handful of letters, and heading home to work from her laptop in between pack-ing—and potion—sessions. But after scanning the first one in the bunch—a note from a sister who was engaged in a family battle over prop-erty inheritance—she'd settled in at her desk for a while.

"Ask Phoebe" is hitting just a little too close to home this week, Phoebe thought. *No pun intended.*

She sighed, propping her glasses back up on her face and fishing another letter out of the pile.

Dear Phoebe,

I have a problem that I hope you can help me with. I don't know where else to turn.

I've been married for three years to the love of my life. My husband and I lived in an apartment for the first two and a half years of our marriage. It was a tight squeeze, but we made it cozy. Still, it was very important to us that we raise our children in a house, and so we saved up our money as best we could.

This past summer, we had finally gotten together enough for a down payment, and we bought the house of our dreams! I was ecstatic, and my husband was too. We moved in three weeks after the paperwork had been approved.

Since then, however, my husband has had lots of trouble sleeping. In fact, I don't think he's made it through a whole night since we've lived here. He complains of recurring nightmares, mostly from his childhood. He and his father used to fight pretty badly.

His nightmares even keep me awake, what with all the tossing and turning. But, of course, that's not the real problem. I just want to help him—help him get through these bad dreams and put his childhood memories behind him.

*He refuses to get counseling. And, other
than being understanding, I'm not sure what's
left for me to do. If you have any advice to offer,
I'd be incredibly grateful—and my husband
would be as well.*

—Hopeless at Home

Little does "Hopeless" know that we've all *got
problems on the homestead these days,* Phoebe
thought, resting her chin in her hand and staring
blankly ahead as she pondered the letter. She
knew that people valued her advice—she had
stacks and stacks of fan mail to prove it—but,
given the trouble that she was having at her own
house, she felt woefully unqualified to dole out
advice on overcoming childhood demons. After
all, wasn't the Manor just spewing her and her
sisters' own demons right back at them? She
sighed.

"Sounds like someone's got the weight of the
world on her shoulders."

She looked up to find Elyse standing in her
doorway. Phoebe shook her head slowly. "I
guess it's not that bad," she said. "But there are
days when giving out advice seems like a really
big responsibility—days when I'm terrified of
saying the wrong thing."

"Look, Phoebe," Elyse said, squaring her
hands on her hips, "no one is perfect. And no

one expects you to have *all* of the answers *all* of the time. The most you can do—the most that you owe your readers—is to speak from your heart. To tell them what you yourself know to be true." She smiled kindly. "I have faith in you. Hey—I'd never have hired you otherwise."

At that, Phoebe couldn't help but laugh. "You know," she admitted, "that actually makes me feel better."

"Good. And now maybe you'll feel a little bit guilty about taking some time off to move," Elyse teased.

Phoebe smirked. "Trust me, I feel guilty enough as it is. You know I'm going to be doing plenty of writing at home."

"I was kidding," Elyse said. "Termites are not something to take lightly. Go home and be with your family."

Phoebe nodded. She gestured toward the pile of papers on her desk. "I will. Of course, that won't solve Hopeless's problem. . . ." She actually felt slightly hopeless herself.

"It'll come to you," Elyse assured her. "Take the letters home. Pack up your house. Reconnect to the things that are true to you. You might be surprised to find your mind cleared."

Phoebe nodded. "You're probably right," she said. "And anyway, it's a start."

After all, what else was there to do?

• • •

Paige knew she was supposed to be packing. Leo was out house hunting and had already found a few perfectly suitable (if charmless) potential homes. Phoebe and Piper were working on putting together a potion and an incantation that would kick-start a housewarming. And everyone had to be out of the house in less than forty-eight hours. Packing was the top priority.

Too bad Paige was preoccupied with other things.

Namely, the alternate-reality TV series unfolding in her bedroom.

The girls had managed to bind whatever blip in the time-space continuum had initially caused the strange manifestations of the other night. But what Paige hadn't told them was that, eventually, the scenes had come back. Apparently, the mojo being worked by the house was industrial strength, and not deterred by a little Power of Three.

Paige had awoken in the middle of the night to see her younger self being taught magic by Grams. She and her three sisters were gathered in the attic, sitting cross-legged on the floor as Grams read from the Book of Shadows.

This scenario was wrong on several levels— especially since Grams, and the girls' mother, had concealed the Halliwell magic from the sisters when they were young. But, once again, it didn't *feel* wrong. It felt like . . . it felt like, for the first time in her life, Paige was finally becoming whole.

She'd been raised by adoptive parents whom

she loved and who loved her, but Paige had always wondered about her birth parents. As a rebellious teen, she'd been devastated by the death of her adoptive parents. She forever regretted having given them a hard time. And meeting her half sisters . . . well, that had been a blessing. But it had also been a challenge. First, she'd had to hop on board with the whole witch-Whitelighter thing. And then there was the question of getting to know her long-lost family. And always feeling like she had to live up to Prue's legacy.

But the faux past that was slowly revealing itself to her acted like a soothing balm on those old wounds. She had a history with her sisters, a bond that belied the actual facts of their upbringing and helped her to find her place with them.

Somewhere in the back of her mind she had a vague sense that her sisters and brother-in-law were off doing things to prepare them all for saying good-bye to their family home. She knew this in the same way that one could see through cotton, or cheesecloth—that is, the knowledge was hazy and intangible, there, but not.

Today, Grams was teaching the three sisters spells for luck. They were to use these spells *only* when helping others—on this subject, Grams was adamant. If they were to use magic to try to create good luck for themselves, the spell could backfire, with disastrous results.

"Personal gain," Real Paige thought to herself,

nodding. When she'd first become a witch, she'd been so excited about her new powers that she had set out to do all sorts of good deeds, with no concern for the potential consequences. Of course, none of her good deeds had gone unpunished. Paige had learned about the ramifications of casting spells for personal gain the hard way.

It would have been nice to have learned that directly from Grams, she thought sadly, watching her young self giggle and rhyme unselfconsciously.

"Luck, pluck, cluck, duck," Young Paige rattled off, ticking off the words on her fingers.

"I don't see how *duck* or *cluck* is going to help us with this spell," Prue said affectionately. She reached out and tousled her sister's hair.

"As a matter of fact, Prue, you might be surprised," Grams interjected. "I'm sure you've heard the expression 'lucky duck,' right?"

Prue nodded vehemently, looking curious.

"Well, how do you think expressions like this become popular?" Grams asked. "There's a reason that the saying exists. One of the key ingredients in a luck-generating spell is duck down."

"Like in pillows," Phoebe offered, her grin revealing gapped teeth. She put her hands precociously on her hips, and eagerly recited:

"Downy duck,
filled with pluck,
release a stroke
of pure good luck!"

"Well, that's just perfect, Phoebe," Grams said, delighted. "You're a natural at writing spells! Now I can teach you girls the potion to go along with the incantation. Come with me down into the kitchen."

Grams held the door open and watched as all four girls scampered out of the attic and down the stairs. She chuckled to herself as they ran by. Then she followed them, closing the door lightly behind her.

Speaking of luck . . . , Paige thought.

It was pretty lucky—to say the least—that she was getting this chance to experience what it would have been like growing up with her birth family. How many people are given the opportunity to *re*experience growing up? Not many, she knew—and certainly not anyone without magical powers working in their favor. And it wasn't something she was going to give up all that easily.

Not at all.

Chapter 6

On the morning of moving day, Piper woke Phoebe much earlier than usual. She tiptoed upstairs and gently tapped her sister on the shoulder until the pretty brunette finally stirred.

"Are you joking?" Phoebe asked groggily. "My alarm hasn't even gone off yet. And the alarm was set for *early*."

"Drink this," Piper said, sliding a mug of steaming, fresh coffee under Phoebe's nose.

Phoebe took a sip and raised an eyebrow at her sister. "Good save," she said. Then she sighed. "I can't believe this day is really here." She glanced around her bedroom, the room that had been hers since childhood. "I can't believe we have to leave the Manor."

"It's only temporary," Piper reminded her. "When we get back, it'll be new and improved. With extra evil-busting power!"

"Why am I not convinced, Pollyanna?" Phoebe asked.

Now Piper sighed. "Oh, who am I kidding? I'm a wreck about this move. At least you've traveled, explored—went off and lived in New York City for a while. I mean, for me, this is the only home I've ever known. *Ever*. You want to know why I'm up so early? It's because I never went to sleep last night. I just tossed and turned for hours, until I finally gave up."

"Poor Piper," Phoebe said. She placed her mug on the nightstand and reached over to give her sister a squeeze. "New York or no, I know exactly how you feel. We just have to keep reminding ourselves that it's only temporary."

"You're right," Piper said. "Do you think you're okay to come downstairs and work with me on the final prep for the cleansing potion? The lavender has been steeping overnight, so it should be ready."

"Of course. Just give me a minute to throw some clothes on and wash my face—the bathroom's safe again, right?" Phoebe asked.

Piper nodded. "For the time being," she said. She yawned and tapped her own coffee mug, peering into it to note that it was, sadly, empty.

"I think I need a refill," she said. "Leo's been with the movers all morning, loading up the van. He'll probably need us to take some boxes, too."

"Phoebe Halliwell, Resident Pack Mule," Phoebe joked, sliding out of bed and rummaging in her closet for a comfy T-shirt and her most broken-in jeans. She quickly pulled her clothes on and laced up some brightly colored tennis shoes. "Look, I'm totally set for some heavy lifting." She paused. "But what do the movers think about your potion?"

"I doubt they've noticed," Piper said. "But even if they have, I think it just looks like I'm brewing some homemade tea." The sisters were fully familiar with the need to be discreet about their witchcraft, and had gotten pretty adept at it.

Phoebe snapped a barrette in her hair, pulling her bangs out of her face. Then she turned back to Piper. "We're going to need the Power of Three for the incantation, right?" she asked.

"Right," Piper confirmed. "I wonder if Paige is up yet."

"I haven't heard her," Phoebe said. "Look, it only takes two of us to finish up the potion. Let her have the extra half hour of sleep. *One* of us should be well rested. We can wake her when we need her."

"You're a good person," Piper said.

"And a *great* sister," Phoebe added, smiling. "Let's go downstairs. I hear that's where the coffee is."

As it happened, Paige was awake—like Piper, she hadn't gone to sleep. She'd spent the night sipping Diet Coke and watching as Grams taught the girls basic spell casting, hexes, charms, and herbal remedies. She'd seen Prue teach Piper how to do a French braid using Young Paige as a model. She'd listened as Prue confessed a crush on a boy in her class, to the horror of all three younger sisters.

She was watching herself grow up.

This morning, Grams was showing Young Paige the secret recipe for her fabulous home-made peanut butter cookies. Prue was out at a birthday party, Piper was at the library, and Phoebe had a playdate. Paige not only had a grandmother to guide her through childhood, but she had her grandmother all to herself—for the morning, at least!

The kitchen itself was a blast from the past. Paige reveled in the old-fashioned appliances, and Grams' prim and proper apron. Young Paige, of course, had smudges of flour across her cheeks, a sure sign of a child enjoying herself in the kitchen.

"You see, Paige, the trick is to use *unsweetened* peanut butter," Grams explained. "The natural kind. Otherwise, you have to watch how much sugar you put in the batter. And who wants to do that?"

Young Paige giggled. "Sugar is good," she said.

Smart kid, Paige reflected. *Though I'm pretty sure that the only way I'd eat unsweetened peanut butter would be in cookie form.*

Young Paige stepped her chubby legs onto a brightly colored stepstool, reaching up on the counter to grab the jar of peanut butter and pass it to Grams.

"Thank you, dear," Grams said, taking the jar from Young Paige's hands. She squinted at the label. "Oh, no," she said. "Looks like I picked up the wrong type of peanut butter at the store. Can you believe it?" She shook her head. "Well, never mind—too late now, I guess," she said. She handed Young Paige a large wooden spoon. "Can you put two scoops of the peanut butter into the mixing bowl?"

Young Paige nodded and did as she was told, clearly thrilled to be helping her grandmother in the kitchen. As she dug her spoon deep into the peanutty goodness, Grams surreptitiously flicked her fingers at the mixing bowl. Real Paige saw a flicker of energy shoot from Grams' fingertips and into the bowl, though Young Paige was none the wiser.

"Personal gain, schmersonal gain," Grams said, laughing quietly to herself.

Young Paige placed her spoon on the ceramic spoon rest atop the kitchen counter. She turned to her grandmother, her eyes open and eager. "Someday, I'll be a mommy," she said, "and I can bake cookies with my children in this kitchen. Just like you and I bake cookies."

Grams smiled and scooped a dollop of batter out of the mixing bowl for Young Paige to sample. "I hope you do," Grams said. "I hope you remember this day, and this special time together."

"Of course I will!" Young Paige exclaimed, indignant. She gobbled down the cookie dough.

"The stuff of childhood can be funny," Grams explained. "It can stay with you forever, or float away. Believe it or not, sometimes it can even turn on you!"

At this, Young Paige looked frightened. Especially since, knowing as she did that magic existed, she had her own ideas about monsters and other frightful scenarios.

Grams smiled reassuringly at Young Paige. "Don't worry," Grams said. "Always remember, as long as you're in this house, you have a haven."

Young Paige wrinkled her nose and nodded, clearly not fully understanding what Grams was trying to say. Real Paige, however, snapped to attention.

Grams is talking to me! Real *me. She's trying to send me a message!*

All at once, Paige's reverie ended. Spots danced before her eyes, like sunspots after looking outside on a bright day, and the scene from her imaginary childhood vanished as though someone had wiped a chalkboard clean. Grams's message was totally and completely clear. Paige knew what had to be done.

Now she just had to convince her sisters.

Paige raced down the stairs to the kitchen. Phoebe and Piper were hunched over the stovetop, tending to a bubbling substance that was obviously the potion they'd be using for the cleansing spell.

"Is that it?" Paige asked, gasping for breath.

Piper looked up. "You're up! And yes, this is it. Almost done. Leo and the movers just drove the van over to the new place, so we've got the house to ourselves. Are you up for a little house-cleaning? Or should I say, house *cleansing*?"

Paige shook her head, feeling slightly desperate. "I don't think so," she said.

"Paige, honey, we're just as bummed about this as you are," Phoebe said gently. "But we have to do it."

"You're not getting me," Paige said impatiently. "I'm not upset about the house. I mean, I *am* upset about the house, but that's not the point right now."

"You realize, you're not making a whole lot of sense, right?" Piper said.

"Listen to me," Paige said. "I talked to Grams." She ignored her sisters' surprised looks and pressed on. "I don't think the house is evil," she insisted. "Grams said this is our haven. It's not that the house has turned on *us*, it's that something evil has taken over the *house*!"

Chapter 7

"Uh, slow down," Piper said, looking intensely suspicious. "In fact, can you do a complete rewind for us? You talked to Grams? When was this?"

Paige colored, slightly embarrassed at what she was going to have to admit to. "It's not so much that I talked to her. Well, I mean, I did, but it wasn't me. Or, it was me, but I was younger. But it was still me, you know?"

Phoebe looked confused. "Sweetie, you're not doing a whole lot to clear any of this up. Grams talked to a *younger*—" She broke off as the realization hit her. "That 'portal to the past' that opened in your room. It's back."

Paige nodded guiltily. "I think it was just temporarily hidden," she admitted. "I just . . . well, I got so caught up in watching my alternate past that I didn't say anything to you. I was afraid you guys would make me bind the portal up again. But I was watching." She swallowed. "The whole time that you guys were packing and working on the potion and the spell, I was watching."

"How did we miss that?" Piper asked, baffled.

"We were pretty caught up in our own stuff," Phoebe reminded her gently. "Memories of growing up in the house. We weren't exactly as alert as we could have been."

"That's just it!" Paige said, growing even more emotional. "I don't have the memories that you guys have here, together. Heck, do you remember how much convincing you had to do to get me to move in here?"

"We do," Phoebe assured her, somewhat playfully. "It'd be pretty hard to forget."

"So, I know the portal was a bad thing—I mean, it was definitely unnatural—but it was . . . I mean, watching myself grow up with you two, and Grams, and Prue? It was pretty cool."

"I guess we can't blame you for getting swept up in false memories," Phoebe said softly. "Especially considering how we've been pretty paralyzed by our own memories lately."

"We should have been paying attention to you," Piper conceded, obviously feeling guilty. "But, come on, Paige—we can't just forget the whole potion and incantation because of some conversation that never even took place. This house is evil. We have to cleanse it if we ever want it to be our home again. Otherwise, we'll have to move out for good."

"I know how you feel, because I was shocked myself," Paige said. "But whether or not I grew up with Grams, the message from her was clear: The house is a haven. It's not evil! She was so determined when she spoke. How could she *not* have been referring to what's going on right now?"

Phoebe glanced at Piper. "I have to admit, I never really thought it made sense, that the Manor would turn on us," she said quietly. "Paige could be on to something."

Piper sighed heavily. "Then what is it? What's going on with the house?"

Paige shook her head. "I wish I knew. But we don't have to move. We just have to get to the bottom of this."

Piper frowned. "I hate to be the holdout, Paige. I mean, I believe that you had some sort of vision last night. But Phoebe and I weren't there. How can we be sure that you were receiving a message from Grams? Maybe it was just your subconscious talking to you."

Paige shrugged, looking increasingly desperate. "You're hesitant—I get that. You *weren't* there. And to be honest, I have no idea why Grams would speak to me rather than to the two of you . . ."

"It could be any number of reasons," Phoebe said quietly. "It could be that maybe Paige was more open to receiving a message than we were. Who knows? But it wouldn't be the first time that one of us clued in to something before the rest of us did."

Piper sighed, placing her hands on her hips. "I trust you, Paige. I'm just worried. The Manor is our touchstone. Whatever course of action we take, it has to be the right one."

"Believe me, I couldn't agree with you more," Paige said, looking solemn.

"Well, what were some of the scenes that you saw last night?" Piper asked, curiosity getting the best of her.

"Hmmm . . ." Paige thought back to the "home movies" she'd been privy to over the course of the night, savoring the images as she conjured them. Her experiences with Grams and her sisters were as meaningful to her now as they'd been when she had first seen them.

"Well, we made peanut butter cookies," Paige said. "Which was super fun. Grams taught me her secret recipe—which, I should add, involved magic."

Phoebe shook her head. "That would never have happened. Personal gain."

"Yeah," Paige said, smiling. "I thought the same thing. But I think her exact words were, 'Personal gain, schmersonal gain.'"

"Okay, I can stop you right there," Piper interjected. "For one thing, Grams was always very careful about personal gain, and for another, her famous cookies weren't peanut butter. They were oatmeal. So your vision must be something that you yourself are projecting. It's obviously not grounded in something real."

"Unless," Paige pointed out, "the message deliberately deviated from reality so that we would all take notice."

"They're both plausible theories," Phoebe agreed. "And personally, I'd rather we exhaust all possibilities before we move out of here."

Piper didn't say anything, but her sisters could tell from her expression that she was starting to come around to their point of view.

Paige stepped over to the range, where Piper had been dutifully stirring the potion.

"May I?" she asked.

Piper nodded, looking only slightly doubtful.

In one fell swoop, Paige scooped up the pot that held the potion, walked it over to the sink, and dumped it unceremoniously down the drain.

"Do we need to rip up the incantation?" Paige asked, dusting off her hands as she replaced the now empty pot to the range.

"I think we're fine just to toss it," Phoebe said. She crumpled her draft into a ball and turned to pitch it into the garbage can, when she noticed that the garbage can was nowhere to be found.

"Scratch that," she said. "Can't toss it in the garbage. The wastebasket is gone. Leo must have loaded it on the van—along with everything else."

"We have to call him!" Paige said, her tone

urgent. "We have to tell him to get the movers to bring all of our stuff back here!"

"I don't think they're going to be too thrilled about that," Piper said dryly.

"Well, we're paying them," Phoebe pointed out. "They're moving the same stuff—just back to the place where they first packed it up." She broke into a dazzling grin. "Piper, you're missing the bigger picture here—we don't have to move!"

"Oh, I get that," Piper said, looking mildly relieved herself. "But here's the thing: Now we've got a whole new can of worms to deal with."

Phoebe and Paige paused, considering this.

"Think about it," Piper continued grimly. "The house isn't evil. That's a good thing. Leo calls the movers, they come back here, we unpack and settle in for another few generations. But *something* has been making this house act out against us, right? So if the house itself isn't evil, what's going on?"

Phoebe and Paige looked at each other helplessly. The plain truth was, they had no idea.

"Okay, Leo and the movers are on their way back here," Piper confirmed, hanging up the cordless phone and turning back to face Paige and Phoebe. "As I predicted, they weren't in love with the idea of hauling everything back here. But, as Phoebe said, we're paying them by the hour, so it's not the end of the world."

"Did Leo think we could be on to something?" Paige asked, worried. She trusted her instincts, but, given her sisters' reluctance, it would be nice to have someone backing her.

Piper sighed. "He admitted that he'd been having a hard time accepting that the house itself was evil. So, even though he hasn't heard anything himself about the house being under the influence of another force, it's a possibility he's willing to consider. *More* than willing," she admitted. "To be honest? I think he's as excited as we are about not having to move."

"Good," Paige said, flopping down on the living room couch exhaustedly.

"I second that," Phoebe said, collapsing next to her. "But now we need a Plan B."

"I agree. I think some recon is in order," Piper suggested. "Research. We should do some digging and try to get some information on the history of the house. Whatever's working against us, there's a good chance it's been here for a while—or else, it's back."

"With a vengeance," Paige added.

"So, newspaper archives, and maybe blueprints of the town," Phoebe said, thinking aloud. "All of which we can find at the library."

"It doesn't open until two," Piper said, glancing at her watch. "Which gives us a few hours to help Leo with boxes."

"Not a problem," Paige joked. "I had planned to spend the day unpacking, anyway."

By two thirty, the movers had returned to the house and dropped off everything that they had only recently packed up. They were in reasonably good spirits, which may have had something to do with the extra tip—and the flirtatious wink and smile—that Phoebe passed along. The girls quickly brought Leo up to speed on the situation.

"So, be honest," Piper implored him after they'd filled him in on Paige's theory. "Do you think we're 100 percent out of our minds for going along with a cryptic message that Paige saw in a vision? Are we totally off base?"

Leo ran his fingers through his short, sandy hair. Moving day was stressful enough without having to worry about messages from the Great Beyond. "I can't say anything for certain," he began, clearly hesitant, "but you three are the Charmed Ones, and if Paige is having any sort of visions, premonitions, or any other kind of magical contact, I don't think we can just ignore it."

"Phoebe's the one who usually gets the premonitions," Piper reminded everyone. "This isn't actually standard operating procedure for us."

"That doesn't change the fact that what Paige saw felt very real to her. Real enough that she called off the move. Which is a pretty big deal," Leo said. "Wouldn't you rather rule out all possibilities before going to the trouble of relocating?"

"We would," Phoebe assured him, shooting a meaningful glance at Piper. "That's why you're here, and so are all of our belongings." She sighed. "Just yesterday, Piper and I were emotional wrecks, wondering what we'd do without the Manor for six months. If there's a chance we don't have to find out, I say we take it."

"Well, that doesn't sound crazy to me," Leo said. "Not at all. *I* wouldn't be here otherwise. You three go and do your research. I can stay with Wyatt."

"Thanks, sweetie," Piper said, grateful. She kissed him on the cheek. "He's napping right now, but you should wake him in half an hour. Otherwise, we'll never get him to sleep tonight."

She turned to her sisters. "Library?"

Phoebe and Paige nodded succinctly, in unison. "Library," they chorused.

The girls grabbed their jackets and keys and headed out.

"Okay," Piper announced, appraising the rows upon rows of bookshelves, card catalogs, and computer monitors. She put her hands on her hips, overwhelmed. "Where do we start?" She turned to Phoebe. "Out of all of us, you were a student the most recently," she said, referring to the fact that Phoebe had gone back to college to get her degree just a few years before.

Phoebe nodded to her sister, surveying the

landscape. "This is a branch library, Piper—it's a lot smaller than the one at school. Its research databases aren't going to be nearly as comprehensive as what I was using back in school."

"Okay, true," Paige said, "but since none of us has a valid student ID, this is as good a place to start as any, right?" She quickly pulled her thick hair into a ponytail, a look that indicated she was ready to get down to work. Her eyes flickered across the main stacks. "You," she began, looking at Phoebe, "check the card catalog—and the Internet—for any urban legends of San Francisco, specifically, anything to do with housing, architecture, or structural integrities. And you," she continued, pointing at Piper, "can check the city hall records for any reported disturbances"—she paused and dropped her voice to a whisper—"that could be linked to the occult."

"Going back how far?" Piper asked, arching an eyebrow warily.

Paige shrugged. "As far back as you can," she said. "We don't have a lot to go on here. We're pretty much shooting in the dark."

"It's a good plan. Or, at least, a good start," Phoebe said, patting Paige on the back supportively. "So I'll be on the computers or"—she gestured with one neatly manicured finger—"over there by the stacks."

"I think there are a few specific computers dedicated to municipal records," Paige said.

"You can ask the woman behind the counter."

Piper peered at the tiny librarian. Her little gray-haired head barely cleared the top of the counter. "That woman probably remembers when each and every record was filed," she observed. "That could be a good thing."

"Never underestimate the value of anecdotal information," Paige agreed.

"Where will you be?" Phoebe asked. "We can't exactly call you if we get separated. They're all about using 'inside' voices here."

"Oh, I'm going to kick it, old-school," Paige said. She nodded her head toward the stairwell. "They keep the microfilm upstairs—every news article printed about this region, ever. Who knows? Maybe there's something about the Manor buried somewhere."

"How come you know the library so well?" Piper asked.

"I quit my day job," Paige reminded her.

Chapter 8

"Well, we made it through at least one night without anything freaky happening to us or to the house," Piper said, smiling at Leo and reaching for a section of the morning newspaper.

The two were enjoying an unusually leisurely breakfast, luxuriating in the fact that, for the past sixteen hours at least, the Manor's manic ways seemed to have settled. Since the wackiness could return at any moment, it was crucial to enjoy the brief respite. Even Wyatt seemed to understand this—he'd slept through the night without so much as a peep. Now he was happily smashing bits of cereal against his high-chair tray with his fist.

"Yeah," Leo agreed. "The good news is that we had a quiet night. The bad news is . . . that we had a quiet night."

"Are you *really* going to rain on my parade?" Piper asked teasingly. "I know, I know," she relented, catching Leo's meaningful look. "It's like the horror movie, when the high school boy says to his very skinny, very blonde girlfriend, 'it's quiet.' And she says—"

"Too quiet," Paige quipped as she came into the kitchen. She went over to the counter to pour herself a glass of orange juice. "Freshly squeezed?" she said, impressed. "Someone here sure slept well!"

"I'll drink to that," Piper said, raising her own glass in Paige's direction. She rolled her eyes. "Though I hate to think that there's such a thing as 'too quiet.'"

"I hear you," Paige said, nodding her head somberly. "But until we've made sense of what we uncovered at the library yesterday, I don't think we can assume anything. Sorry, sis. Wish it were another way."

"Well, Phoebe took advantage of being well rested and left for the office early," Piper said. "Something about needing to do a little 'face time.'"

"Ah, office-speak—I get it," Paige said. "Seeing as how our schedules are so . . . erratic. Makes it hard to hold down a grown-up job. That's why I don't try to anymore." She grinned, making it clear that she was perfectly happy with her decision.

"Anyway, she said she had a mountain of letters to get to, but that she would definitely carve out some time to look over her research," Piper said. "I've got my own avalanche of printouts to deal with."

"I put them on the dining room table for you," Leo chimed in helpfully. "But I *will* move them to the coffee table in the living room," he quickly amended, seeing Piper's glare.

"Thanks, sweetie," she said. "I think just the one magical labor is plenty for me right now. I'm not going near that dining room until we're sure we've washed the wonky magic right out of these floorboards."

"So you're going to read your stuff today, and you'll be able to go over it all tonight—like, say, after dinner?" Paige asked, eager to confirm the plan.

"I will get on it first thing today," Piper said, holding up one hand in a "Scout's honor" salute. She started, seeing her wristwatch and noting the time. "Correction: I will get on it *second* thing today. Wyatt and I have Mommy and Me in an hour."

Paige shot Piper a look. "Mommy and Me? Piper, we almost had to move yesterday—for six months! Don't you think we've maybe got some other stuff on our plate?"

"Yeah, I do," Piper agreed. "And that's kind of exactly the point. Our home life has been anything but stable lately. Between his own random acts of magic, and the Manor freaking out on us, it's been pretty chaotic for us—*all* of us. That includes Wyatt. We're the Charmed Ones, sure. We know the drill. But he's too young to really understand what's going on. And I'm going to do everything in my power to help him live as

normal a life as possible, that's for darned sure."
She folded her arms across her chest, looking
somewhat more defensive than she intended.

"If it makes you feel any better, Paige, I was
going to interview the Elders about the history
of the Manor while Piper's gone," Leo offered
helpfully.

Paige opened her mouth as though to protest,
then closed it abruptly, clearly thinking better of
it. From his seat next to Piper at the breakfast
table, Leo nodded subtly.

Paige's expression softened. "You're right,"
she conceded. "I'm constantly going on about
how we have to balance being witches with
being people." She reached over to tussle the
few hairs on Wyatt's head. "That totally goes
double for my nephew." She turned to Piper, her
hazel eyes bright and earnest.

"Have a great time," she said.

"Having a good time?" Celeste, the mother host-
ing this morning's Mommy and Me class,
chirped brightly at Piper.

As a general rule, Piper was fairly opposed to
people who chirped, but it was so refreshing to
be doing something relaxing and normal with
her son that, instead, she only beamed in reply.
"I sure am—and Wyatt is too," she said, pointing to a spot on the ground a few feet away
where Wyatt was playfully menacing another
child with a stuffed tiger.

She surveyed the rec room, which was a
deluxe, supersized space that rivaled most
theme parks. The walls had been painted in
bright primary colors and the floor was covered
in thick, plush carpeting. An enormous flat-
screen TV hung on the far wall, broadcasting the
latest in educational kiddie programming—with
the sound turned down. Celeste had thought-
fully—and creatively—sectioned off the room
into different stations: building blocks in one
corner, plush toys in another. She'd even had the
foresight to set up a few easels, complete with
smocks and watercolor paints, for the more
intrepid older attendees. Wyatt and Piper were
in Mommy and Me heaven, and it looked like
everyone else was too.

Score one point for "normal," Piper thought,
pleased.

"Do you think it's too early to put out
snacks?" Celeste wondered aloud.

Piper waved her hand dismissively. "*Please.*
It's never too early to put out snacks!" she
insisted. "I used to be a professional chef—do
you need a hand with the graham crackers?" She
leaned in conspiratorially. "Seriously, I'm a whiz
at opening boxes. That kind of training? It never
leaves you."

Celeste laughed. "Well, everything's all laid
out in the kitchen, but if you're offering to help
tote . . ."

Piper nodded. "I live to serve."

"Can you work weeknights, too?" Celeste asked teasingly. She beckoned in the direction of the kitchen. "Follow me."

"Right behind you," Piper assured her.

Which was when she heard the tigerish growl.

"Okay," she said to herself. "That's not really the type of noise you want to be hearing at your son's playgroup."

She whirled to face the playroom again, accurately sensing that Wyatt had something to do with this recent visit from the wild kingdom.

"Of course," she murmured, seeing the slavering, menacing tiger slink out of the corner and toward the center of the room.

For his part, Wyatt, from his perch in the designated "plush area" of the room, had the good grace to look somewhat abashed.

Piper had to think fast. First things first: Had anyone else noticed the tiger yet?

Thankfully, it looked as though they hadn't. The sensory overload that was the playroom was therefore doubly appreciated, at least as far as Piper was concerned. The stereo, which had seemed so quiet just moments ago, suddenly sounded incredibly loud and incredibly earnest. It seemed to be drowning out most of the noise made by the tiger.

Which, it appeared, was headed directly toward Piper.

"That works out well," she mused.

In a flash, she extended her fingers and froze the room. Mothers and toddlers alike paused mid–bonding activity. Only Wyatt remained animated, obviously delighted at the appearance of the tiger-demon, and obviously doing his best to mask his glee.

His best, Piper noted dryly, was not all that impressive.

"Nice one, kid," she said. "I've got to hand it to you—you've got a real knack for this stuff."

Wyatt giggled and clapped his hands.

Piper knew that the two of them weren't in any immediate danger. After all, Wyatt had proven himself time and again to be the best supernatural protection plan a mother could possibly have. When pressed, he was just as helpful as the Charmed Ones in a battle. Sometimes even more so.

But, then again, the tiger-demon didn't look all that friendly. And, considering she still had a scratch on her arm from her encounter with the supersized puppy, a little caution was probably in order.

Its upper lip (*Do tigers have lips?* Piper wondered, before pushing the thought out of her mind to attend to more urgent matters) was curled into a nasty-looking sneer, and a thin line of drool was making its way down his chin (*Do tigers have chins?*). His legs moved forward with well-oiled precision, his body sleek and well muscled.

This was not good.

The tiger-demon tensed, ready to spring. Piper reacted with equal precision.

"Here, kitty, kitty," she coaxed, beckoning with one finger.

The tiger-demon opened its mouth, revealing glistening fangs. It reared back on its hindquarters, panting and snorting.

"I have to tell you—not your most attractive look," Piper said.

And with flick of her wrist, the tiger was gone.

"I hope everyone had a good time today," Celeste said, passing out homemade chocolate-chip cookies that she'd baked and wrapped in individual bunches as favors for her Mommy and Me guests.

"Absolutely," Piper said, echoing the genuine enthusiasm she'd displayed in earlier, simpler, pre-tiger times. "You have a great house for this sort of thing."

"You do," said Holly, another mother who was on her way out, daughter Melanie, a striking redheaded toddler, in tow. "The stations were the perfect touch. Melanie just loves to watercolor." She held up a few dried paintings that Melanie had done over the course of the afternoon for emphasis. "She's my little Monet," Holly said. "Or, should I say, Mon-*ette*."

"She's gorgeous," Piper said, smiling.

"She takes after her father," Holly confided, hugging Melanie against her legs. "So . . . do we know where we're having this next week?" The mothers rotated hostessing duties.

"Oh, I'm not sure. I don't think anything was decided," Piper said. She didn't want to be rude, but she was determined to keep a close eye on Wyatt until she got him back home. She couldn't exactly concentrate on anything the other mommies were talking about when she was worried about having to mop up another supernatural spill!

"Well, I'd be more than happy to do it," Holly said, smiling graciously—and pointedly—in Piper's direction, "but I really don't want to step on anyone's toes—"

"No! No toe stepping," Piper said, jumping in almost too quickly. She took a deep breath to calm herself before continuing. "You should definitely host next week's Mommy and Me if you want. Absolutely." She made the "cross my heart" gesture with the hand that wasn't holding Wyatt.

"Are you sure?" Holly said. "Because we would all just love to come to your place. I know it for a fact. The mommies were all just saying—"

"Please, host!" Piper said. "We're having some . . . work done right now, so the house isn't in the best shape. But you know I'd love to host whenever."

●   ●   ●

For Phoebe, "face time" at work was proving a bit more challenging than she'd expected. To the left of her double-tall soy latte stood a stack of letters so high it rivaled a Ph.D. dissertation. To the right, a ream of printouts from the library so prodigious that it almost made her dizzy.

At least the house was quiet last night, and I could get some sleep, she mused. *How does the expression go? Thank goodness for small favors?*

A few rounds of training in the Manor basement would have helped her to relieve some stress, but something told her that the basement wouldn't be the best place to work out just now. She'd have to settle for some cardio boot camp at the local fitness center later on.

That is, if I can ever get through any of this, and get out of here. She ran her fingers through her short, dark hair and sighed, feeling overwhelmed.

Her work—what of it she'd done—hadn't been completely in vain, thankfully. She'd been at the office since the crack of oh-my-lord, shocking the morning janitor with a sunny, if slightly sleepy, smile upon her arrival. She'd since made it through maybe a quarter of the printouts she'd gotten from the library, mostly news stories of wacky events that had taken place in or near the Manor.

If people only knew, Phoebe thought, smiling to herself. And, given the history of completely bizarre occurrences within the vicinity of the Manor, it was a wonder that they weren't more suspicious.

It's because there are witches like us—and friends like Darryl—to handle the damage control.

With another deep sigh, she flipped through the clippings again.

> *August 4, 1926*
> *Authorities were shocked to discover an influx of rare gray doves clustered in the front yard of this Bay Area home. . . . It has been reported that the birds appeared "overnight, like magic," though, of course, their natural habitat is generally found in enclaves of the Northeastern coast.*

> *October 28, 1939*
> *Though the next lunar eclipse is not predicted until the year 1955, it has been reported that last night, at approximately 3:21 a.m., the moon was nearly completely obscured by lunar cloud cover and rendered invisible to the naked eye. "It was like somethin' Nostradamus would have predicted," a local is quoted as saying, "like the end of the world." However, just as quickly as the moon had been covered, it reappeared, leaving most meteorologists and astronomers baffled at what they had seen.*

> *April 29, 1967*
> *This quiet, unassuming Bay Area residential block awoke this morning to find the street blanketed in a dusting of ash. To the best of every-*

one's knowledge, there had been neither fire nor smoke over the course of the night, raising the question of just where, exactly, the ash did originate.

Phoebe couldn't help but smile to herself as she flipped through the clippings. There were dozens, spanning the ages since the Manor had first been built. Reading through the news articles was like a history lesson in her Charmed ancestry. Each of these "unexplained incidents," she knew, had very obvious—if completely supernatural—explanations. Dove feathers, for instance, were known for their calming powers, and were therefore used in many peace-granting potions. Temporary lunar eclipses were actually common in times of strife between good magic and evil. And heavy ash was a common byproduct of much spell casting.

The Halliwell witches have been practicing magic—and making their home—at the Manor throughout the ages, Phoebe mused, feeling a slight shiver go down her spine. Unlike her sisters Prue and Piper, Phoebe had been the first to discover their Charmed heritage, and the most eager to look into reclaiming their bound powers. Being a Charmed One sworn to save Innocents was incredibly demanding, of course, but she wouldn't have traded her sacred responsibility for anything. Reading about the history of her family only strengthened that resolve.

Of course, I'm also responsible for helping people in less witchy ways, she realized, glancing with dismay at the many, many letters from readers of "Ask Phoebe." She plucked one from the top of the pile. After all, there was a reason she'd come into work today.

Dear Phoebe,

I've got a problem that I was hoping you could help me with. My husband thinks I'm being kind of immature, so a second opinion would definitely be appreciated.

I recently returned home for my thirty-year high school reunion. Just going home for the reunion was pretty stressful, I have to admit, but for me there was the added strain of staying with my mother, who, until that weekend, I'd seen only occasionally over the past fifteen years.

You see, my husband and I moved from Nebraska—where I grew up—to San Francisco just after we were married, and though we're very happy here, money is tight. So we don't get back to visit my mother as often as we'd like.

My mother doesn't like the situation very much, and I think she harbors even more resentment than she admits to. So, when I went home for my reunion, I wasn't com-

pletely surprised to find that she had turned my childhood bedroom into a sewing room! (My husband and I slept on the pullout couch in the living room.)

No, her renovating my bedroom didn't bother me. What did bother me, though, is that she apparently gave away all of my childhood toys to Goodwill—without even asking me first! When I told her how upset that made me, she was dismissive, saying that they'd only been taking up space.

Now, I know that she has a point, but my point is, those toys were my memories! Even if she doesn't have the space to keep them in her house, I wish she had offered me the chance to take them off her hands. My beloved teddy, which my parents had given to me on my fourth birthday, is now gone forever, along with many other pieces of my childhood.

I've tried talking to my mother calmly, Phoebe, but she just doesn't understand. What do you think? Am I being unreasonable? I'd love to hear from you.

Thanks,
Sentimental in San Francisco

After reading the letter, Phoebe paused to marvel at how the problems of her readers so closely paralleled the trauma that she was experiencing in her own life. Charmed or not, she realized, people's attachments to their homes, their childhoods, and their memories were strong indeed. How could she accuse "Sentimental" of overreacting when she and her sisters were having a similar response to what was going on in their own home?

Speaking of her own home, she was eager to get back to it—maybe more eager now than she'd been before. She thought for a beat, then hunched over her keyboard to draft reply to the letter.

> *Dear Sentimental,*
>
> Unreasonable *is a pretty strong term for some very basic human emotions!*
>
> *While I can see your husband's and your mother's point—after all, if the toys meant so much to you, why were they being kept at your mom's house rather than at yours?—I do understand the powerful connection you feel to your memories. It certainly would have been nice if your mother had thought to offer the toys to you before donating them to charity.*
>
> *It may be little comfort, but the truth is, now that your toys have been handed off to Goodwill, you're giving other children a chance to make memories of their own. Which, as you yourself know, can be incredibly forma-tive.*
>
> *In the meantime, maybe a good idea would be to focus on other ways to forge a connection*

with your mother—ways that don't cost as much money as a plane ticket—and to make new memories that the two of you will be able to savor for years to come!

Phoebe exhaled and read the letter over quietly to herself once or twice, rubbing her eyes from the glare of the computer screen. She couldn't help but wonder if she was too attached to this particular subject matter, if maybe her advice wasn't as unbiased as it should have been. But there wasn't a lot of time to dwell on the thought. This one letter that she had answered was just a tiny, tiny drop in the bucket. She still had floods of material to get through.

She glanced at the clock and was surprised at the late hour. It looked like she wouldn't be getting to those floods until another day.

Back to my own house, she thought, scooping up her keys and other personal detritus that cluttered the surface of her desk. She powered down her laptop and slipped it into its sleeve.

"I'm home," Phoebe called, dropping her bag and keys onto the console table in the front hall as she closed the door behind her. "I am thrilled to report that face time is officially over for the day. Now I can fully dedicate myself to 'house time.' You guys are gonna love the stuff that I've dug up on the Manor. Let there be no doubt—Halliwells have been making their homes here for many, many generations."

"I, for one, never doubted it," Paige called from the living room. "But I'd love to see what you turned up." Ever since she had embraced her heritage, Paige was particularly interested in learning more about what it meant to be a witch. So this exercise in delving deeper into the roots of the Manor was especially fascinating to her.

Phoebe wandered into the living room with copies of the clippings she'd found in hand. She knew Paige would definitely appreciate some of the more bizarre stories she'd uncovered. "Here," she said, placing a stack on the coffee table in front of where Paige sat. "Better than *US Weekly*." She paused for a moment, taking in the quiet of the early evening. "Awfully peaceful around here," she mused. "Where is everybody?"

"Piper and Wyatt were at Mommy and Me," Paige said, frowning slightly. She'd gotten the full rundown from Piper when Piper had first come home.

"Let me guess—it didn't go totally smoothly?" Phoebe ventured.

"Wyatt does like to exercise his powers when he has the opportunity," Paige replied. "Let Piper fill you in later. Anyway, mommy and baby are both upstairs taking a nap. And Leo is up interviewing the Elders. He's hoping that they might have more insights, now that we have a slightly different lead on what might be causing all the weirdness around here."

"Has there been anything new?" Phoebe asked.

"Thankfully, no," Paige said. "Although—" She broke off, cocking her head to one side. "Did you hear that?"

Phoebe peered at her. "No. I heard nothing. Other than you speaking, of course."

Paige shook her head. "Huh. Must be my imagination." She squinted. "I could swear, though . . ." She paused again. "You really don't hear that? The whispering? The buzzing sound?"

Still squinting, Paige leaned to one side, as though in the direction that the sound was coming from. "Okay, I know you're going to think that I've officially lost my mind," she told Phoebe, who was looking increasingly confused as the moments ticked by, "but I'm telling you, I hear whispers. Quiet, rushing, horror-movie whispers." She took a few tentative steps toward the breakfront that stood against the wall, as though she thought she might be getting warmer.

She stopped, looking horrified. "It's *that*," she gasped, pointing at a photograph of Phoebe, Piper, and Prue from a Christmas many, many years past. "The photo is whispering to me!"

"Really?" Phoebe said, equal parts shocked and dubious. "What's it saying?"

Paige shook her head. "I can't make out actual words. But the tone is . . . sinister. Like there's a cloud of evil around the picture, and the memory."

"If there were an evil aura surrounding the photo, don't you think I would have picked up on it, sweetie?" Phoebe pointed out gently. "I mean, I *am* the empath, and I'm the sister who's known for having premonitions."

"True, but I'm the one who had a portal to the past suddenly appear in her bedroom," Paige reminded her. "Whatever is haunting the Manor, I don't think it's exactly playing by the rules." She sighed. "The whispering is getting louder. It's pretty hard to ignore." Her eyes widened as another thought occurred to her. "If this keeps up, I'll have a heck of a time helping you guys deal with whatever is possessing the house."

"Which is probably just what it wants—whatever *it* is," Phoebe said. Her mouth set in a tight little line. She glanced upward and put her hands on her hips. "Leo!" she called, determined. "We need you!"

Leo appeared in a shower of twinkling light. He looked confused, and more than a little bit concerned. "What's going on?"

"Did you get anything from the Elders?" Phoebe asked.

He shook his head. "I have confirmation of the generations of witches that have lived in the Manor, and I can probably corroborate whatever research you three have pulled from the library. But nothing like this has ever happened in the Manor before. So they're at a loss."

"Oh, that is *so* not helpful," Paige moaned. "Okay, forget that for a minute. Listen." She cocked her head again, silent, indicating for Leo to follow her lead.

"What am I supposed to be listening to?" he asked, puzzled.

Paige assumed an exasperated pose. "Okay, so it's just me, then. I *am* completely and totally losing my mind. Awesome." Her mock tirade over, she turned toward Leo again. "It's the picture. It's crying out to me. And I don't know what to do about it."

Leo looked thoughtful, then opened his mouth as if to speak. He didn't get very far, however, before he was interrupted by a loud clanging noise from upstairs.

"What was that?" Phoebe asked, worried.

"I'll let you know," Leo said, orbing upstairs in a flash of white light.

Paige and Phoebe were hot on his heels. Paige grabbed her sister by the wrist and the two of them orbed up into Piper and Leo's bedroom. What they saw there was incredibly disturbing.

One by one, the books on Piper's bookshelves were flying off the shelves and onto the floor. Once they were all collected in a heap, they reversed their trajectory and realigned themselves on the shelves. Then they came shooting off all over again. Proust, Danielle Steele, Stephen King, Salman Rushdie . . .

classics, chick lit—all different genres shot up and down with the force of a cannonball.

Fortunately, Piper seemed safe enough on the bed. None of the books reached her as they launched themselves from the shelves. But they made a huge clatter as they landed on the floor, and there was no telling what, if any, other objects would be next.

But that wasn't even the worst part.

"Oh, my God!" Phoebe cried, once she'd fully taken in the scene in front of her. "Leo, what *happened*?"

"Not sure," Leo said wryly. "But I *think* my orbing is on the fritz."

"Really?" Piper asked, arching an eyebrow. "What would make you say that?"

She was obviously being sarcastic: While Leo's upper body—his head, torso, and arms—had made its way into the bedroom, his legs had somehow been left behind.

"Uh, guys?" Paige began nervously, "I know we've got other things to worry about right now, but . . ." She pointed.

Everyone followed the direction of her gaze. The books from the bookshelves had now begun launching themselves straight across the room and toward Wyatt's crib—whereupon they bounced harmlessly off his force field. A Jane Austen boxed set was being particularly tenacious, but, thankfully, it couldn't do any damage.

"Okay, well, nice to know that, as usual, my son can take care of himself," Piper observed. "But I do think that we are under some kind of house arrest that needs to be dealt with—stat."

"The attic?" Paige asked. "Seems like that's our safe room right now."

"So the Manor has succeeded in corralling us in the attic?" Phoebe asked. "I mean, what—are we going to sleep there?"

"If we have to," Leo said. "I can't orb properly, Paige is hearing voices, and Piper's bedroom has gone into attack mode. I'd say we're safest up there until we've gotten things a little more under control."

The popping sound that the books made as they collided with Wyatt's force field reminded the girls that time was of the essence. *Sense and Sensibility* would not be ignored.

"Okay," Phoebe said reluctantly. "I'll round up some blankets and pillows for us. Piper and Paige, you're okay getting Wyatt up into the attic?"

Paige mock saluted. "Aye-aye."

"And Leo . . . well, just orb as much of yourself as you can up into the attic. Hopefully, the influence of the Book will have some effect on you, and it will be easier to figure out how to get the rest of you upstairs."

"Sounds like a plan," Piper said, warily eying the books as they floated their way back up to the bookshelves. "Let's get on it."

• • •

Unfortunately, the Book of Shadows didn't seem to contain any references to orbing mishaps. It looked like Leo and the sisters were on their own.

"I come bearing bedding," Phoebe said, marching into the attic with her arms full of sheets and a determined look etched across her delicate features.

"Anything happen while you were downstairs?" Piper asked.

Phoebe shook her head. "Uh-uh. The lending library in your bedroom looks to be under control. Maybe it was just waiting for us to leave?"

"Great," Piper said, scowling. "So my own belongings have succeeded in chasing me out of my bedroom. Fabulous."

"Yeah, it's a problem," Phoebe agreed. "But, right now? I think we've got some other problems that deserve your attention. Like, for example, how your husband's gone all Humpty-Dumpty on us. And we need to put him back together again."

Leo offered a strained smile and placed his hands on his hips, then dropped them back at his sides when he realized that most of his hips were still downstairs in the living room. "Suggestions welcome," he said.

"Well, the Book is no help," Paige said, exhaling deeply in frustration. "Why don't we try a spell?"

"Good idea," Phoebe said, nodding thought-fully. She concentrated for a moment, scanning her brain for some workable rhymes. "Whole . . . mole . . . foal . . ."

"Keep thinking, Sis," Piper offered.

Suddenly, a gleam came into Phoebe's eyes. She clapped her hands enthusiastically. "Come on—let's grab hands and form a circle around Leo."

The sisters did as they were told, pausing to pass Wyatt to the safety of his father's arms. Once they were in formation, Phoebe closed her eyes and indicated that her sisters should do the same. Satisfied that they were all as ready as they were going to get, she began a quick chant:

> *"We three sisters, body and soul,*
> *request our angel be made whole."*

The girls waited for a beat, then cautiously peeled open first one eye, then the other. Miraculously, Leo was back in one piece!

"Thank goodness!" Piper said, pulling Leo toward her to embrace him. "I kind of prefer you this way—you know, with arms *and* legs."

"Yeah, four appendages seem to work best," Leo agreed, smiling with relief. "I do wish we knew what had caused that, though."

"Probably the same thing that's causing everything else around here," Paige ventured.

"Whatever is possessing the house is preventing you from orbing. Or, at least, preventing *all* of you from orbing."

"What now?" Phoebe asked, clearly flummoxed.

"I have a crazy idea," Piper began. "How about we hit the sack?"

"Now?" Phoebe asked in disbelief. "It's only"—she quickly checked her wristwatch—"eight thirty. I don't even think I'll be able to sleep at this hour!"

"You might surprise yourself," Paige said, yawning broadly. "Now that Piper mentions it, I'm exhausted. Maybe it *is* best to call it a day."

"Agreed," Leo said, starting toward the pile of sheets and blankets and laying them out in as comfortable an arrangement as he could. "We can get an early start tomorrow, when we're fresh." He seemed somewhat pleased to be making use of his whole body, now that he could.

"Obviously, I'm outvoted," Phoebe said, sighing resignedly. "Or maybe I'm just not too eager to camp out in the attic."

"None of us are, sweetie," Piper said. "But for tonight, I think it's safest."

"Safety in numbers," Paige echoed. "And, you know, sleeping in the shadow of . . . the Book of Shadows."

"You're not kidding," Phoebe grumbled, shimmying under a thick blanket and pulling it up to her chin. "This is really . . . cozy." She looked around. "Maybe we could move some chairs, and that old trunk over there?" she asked, pointing. "It would give us a little more room, don't you think?"

"Good call," Leo said, bounding up to do as Phoebe had suggested. "Listen, it could be worse," he continued, trying to look on the bright side. "It's a little cramped up here, but it definitely could be worse."

"Are you *trying* to jinx us?" Piper asked Leo teasingly.

"You're right. I take it back," he amended hastily. "It's cramped, we'll live, sleep tight."

"Don't let the bedbugs bite!" Paige replied with false cheer.

Then she turned out the lights.

"Okay, someone didn't get the memo about it being an early bedtime tonight," Piper said, half teasing, half anxious, as she hovered over Wyatt's bassinette. He'd been crying for the better part of an hour, what began as measured whines steadily building into full-fledged shrieks. Piper had tried cradling him, she'd walked him around the attic, and each of the sisters as well as Leo had taken a turn at singing to the toddler, all to no avail. As Wyatt's cries grew louder and louder, his face became redder and redder.

"This is a problem," Phoebe said. "My nephew is turning into a tomato. An incredibly sad, yet still amazingly cute, tomato." She leaned over Wyatt, who was flailing inconsolably in Piper's lap. "What is it, baby?

Tell us what's wrong so that we can help you."

"He can't be hungry," Piper said, "since he's already eaten. He doesn't need to be changed—I checked."

"And I double-checked," Paige added. "That's definitely not our problem."

"This is horrible," Piper fretted. "I hate to see him so distraught. And if we can't figure out what's wrong with him, none of us is going to be very happy tonight."

She mentally ticked off the things that Wyatt needed for bedtime. "Dinner, check. Clean diaper, check. Bath—well, we had to put it off, but something tells me that's not what's got him so freaked out. . . ."

"He might be upset that he's sleeping in the bassinette and not in his regular crib," Phoebe suggested. In their haste, the sisters had eschewed bringing the crib upstairs, since dragging it up the old-fashioned way would have been a struggle, and neither Paige nor Leo trusted their orbing at the moment.

Piper shook her head. "That's never been a problem before."

"He has his pacifier and his blankie," Paige said. "I know he can't fall asleep without those."

"Bobo!" Piper called out in a flash of inspiration. "He needs Bobo!"

Phoebe smacked her palm to her forehead in a classic "duh" gesture. "I can't believe I left that downstairs," she said. "Once I'd grabbed the bassinette, I sort of stopped thinking. Sorry." She shrugged sheepishly. "There was a lot going on."

Bobo was a bug-shaped toy that Wyatt adored. It had six legs, with a different apparatus affixed to each leg. Bobo spent most of his time in Wyatt's crib, because Wyatt loved to play quietly with Bobo just before he fell asleep each night.

"It must still be in his crib," Leo said. "I can go down and get it."

"That's okay," Piper said. "I think I might need to stretch my legs, anyway. Here," she continued, handing her son off to her husband, "you take him while I run downstairs."

"Are you sure?" Leo asked.

Piper nodded. "Look, if you go downstairs, we can't guarantee that you'll come back in one piece, right?"

Leo smiled. "I wasn't planning on orbing."

Piper waved his protests away. "I'll be back in a flash," she promised. "You won't even notice I'm gone."

Back in a flash, Piper thought grimly to herself as she cautiously tiptoed down the hall. *You won't even notice I'm gone.* At that very moment, the house seemed settled, but every muscle in her body was tensed for another surprise.

She paused at the door to her and Leo's bedroom, squeezing her eyes shut and taking a deep breath. Then, with a burst of energy, she grabbed the handle and pushed the door open.

Nothing.

"Nothing," Piper mused aloud. "I could get into nothing. Nothing is nice. And *quiet*."

She walked across the floor to Wyatt's crib and peered in. Bobo wasn't immediately visible, so she reached in and began groping around. *Rattle, no, fuzzy bear, no—Bobo!* Piper's hands wrapped around the toy triumphantly.

Which was when the closet door burst open.

At first, Piper wasn't sure what she was seeing. The creature that emerged from the closet was an amorphous blob, something shapeless and almost colorless, save for two dull, beady, coal-colored eyes set deep into its boneless figure.

Also, it had fangs. Sharp, pointed fangs that glistened with drool. And while its expression was difficult to read in the semidarkness, Piper didn't have to think too hard to guess what those fangs were for.

The better to eat you with, my dear.

The creature began to lumber toward her, snarling and slavering. Its girth made it slow, which gave Piper a chance to think. She reached out and flashed the fingers of one hand at it.

With a poof, a small black scorch mark appeared in the wall behind the monster. The creature itself remained unharmed.

"Yeah, that's a problem," Piper quipped.

She tried again.

Nothing.

Well, not nothing. A painting hung on the wall shattered on impact, its frame sliding off its hook and crashing onto the floor.

"Oh, oops!" Piper exclaimed.

Now the creature emitted a low rumbling sound. Was it . . . *laughing* at her?

"Oh, no," Piper said, still speaking more to herself. "Now, that is just unacceptable."

Obviously, blowing the creature up was going to take a little extra effort, though Piper had no idea why. She wracked her brain for a beat or two, then looked squarely at the demon.

"Here goes nothing," she muttered.

> *"Creature from the closet,*
> *demon from beyond,*
> *this Charmed One commands you—*
> *Be gone!"*

She dropped Bobo to the ground and flung her arms outward with all of her might, feeling the magic course through her and out the tips of her fingers.

The stream of power hit the demon with a mighty sound, almost like the *thwack* of an electrical shock magnified a million times. Piper reeled backward from the impact. For a moment, the room was clouded with smoke, and there was a faint odor of ozone, or gasoline.

The creature was gone.

Piper dusted herself off, pulling her hair back

from her flushed face. She reached down and plucked Bobo from the floor. She regarded the toy with skepticism.

"Let's hope you were worth all the trouble," she said.

Then she made her way back up to the attic.

Chapter 9

"I found Bobo," Piper said wearily, stepping into the attic and shutting the door behind her. "It was, um, easier said than done."

"We gathered as much when we heard the crashing sounds from downstairs," Phoebe said, rushing to her sister's side. "Piper, is everything okay?"

"Everything's fine—now," Piper said. "Emphasis on *now*. Let's just say that there was a little surprise waiting for me in the bedroom closet."

"Wait—you're telling us you were attacked by a closet monster?" Phoebe asked, her disbelief etched across her face.

"Yeah," Piper said, shrugging. "Given everything else that's been going on around here, I don't get why that's so hard for you to believe."

"No," Phoebe said, running her fingers through her hair. Her eyes twinkled excitedly.

"It's not hard for me to believe at all—Piper, don't you get it?"

Piper shot her sister a look. "Clearly not. Help me out here, Phoebes."

Phoebe shook her head. "I can't believe that you don't remember. Though I guess that's a good thing—it means you've matured. The *Closet Monster*? Piper, come on! When you were little, you were terrified of that thing. Prue managed to convince us that it was real. I think you must've been about six. For, like, a year you wouldn't go anywhere near your closet. Mom said it was impossible to get you dressed in the morning."

Piper's bright brown eyes registered shock as memory surfaced. "You're totally right. It's all coming back to me." She grew excited. "It's incredible that I blocked that out!" She sighed. "Well, I guess that means that our most recent demon is in keeping, thematically, with everything else that's been going on in the house."

"Yeah, it's all of our childhood memories acting out against us," Paige mused. "Of course, we still have no idea why." She sighed. "That's the tricky part."

Leo yawned. "Listen, now that the Closet Monster—and Piper's childhood traumas—have been dispensed with, I say we go back to plan A. I think a good night's sleep is probably the first step toward figuring out what's possessed the house, and vanquishing it for good."

"Hear, hear," Piper said, brandishing Bobo like a champagne flute. "And, here, here," she continued, walking over to the bassinette and placing Bobo inside. "Look, Wyatt," she cooed, her features softening at the sight of her son, "look at what Mommy found for you."

Up until this point, Wyatt's cries had mostly subsided to the level of the occasional sniffle. Now that he had Bobo back, however, he began shrieking at full volume all over again. His reaction was exactly the opposite of what the sisters and Leo expected, as his face became beet-red and his little lungs began working overtime.

"Or not?" Piper asked, puzzled. "I don't get it. I was so sure that Bobo was what he wanted."

"Well, he doesn't seem to want it now, that's for sure," Paige observed. "That, or he just has a funny way of showing affection."

Indeed, Wyatt was kicking his feet and shrinking as far away from the offending critter as he possibly could. He certainly didn't seem happy to see Bobo. In fact, if anything, he seemed more distraught than ever to be anywhere near the toy.

"Yeah, this isn't working," Piper said. "Which means I'm fresh out of solutions." She leaned in toward Wyatt. "Sweetie, what is it?"

By way of response, Wyatt grabbed Bobo with one chubby little fist, and tossed him overboard.

Bobo hit the floor.

And then everything changed.

• • •

As Bobo landed on the floor, the sisters and Leo reeled back in a flash of light. When they opened their eyes again, Bobo stood before them—in demon form.

Paige blinked and whispered to Phoebe, "I think I liked him better when he was just a toy."

"Ya think?" Phoebe asked dryly.

Demon Bobo stood at least eight feet tall, his eyes flashing with rage and his tentacles swinging in every direction. The girls bobbed and weaved as they assessed the situation.

"Okay, people, I think we've got a problem here," Piper ventured.

Now that he was corporeal, Bobo was a lot less appealing, and his various buggy tentacles were much more menacing.

"So, uh, what's that?" Paige asked, pointing at a pinching claw that crept toward the sisters with an intent that was, without a doubt, not good.

"Pincher," Piper said simply. "It was a lobster claw when Bobo was stuffed. It was actually kind of cute."

The pincher snapped at Piper, missing her arm by an inch.

"Okay, I'm minus one sleeve," she groused. "*Now* it's personal."

She reached out and flicked her arms toward the demon, then reeled back, bracing herself for the shock of the explosion.

But the explosion never came.

The surge of magic from Piper's fingertips shot into the lobster claw and rattled off harmlessly, a stream of power not unlike electricity running up and down Bobo's arm. Bobo glanced down at his arm, looking more annoyed than anything else.

"What is he, ten feet tall now?" Phoebe wondered aloud. She shuddered. "Very creepy. Wyatt's childhood fears are almost as bad as ours are."

"Less joking, more vanquishing," Piper suggested.

"What am I supposed to d—"without finishing her sentence, Phoebe levitated into the air like something out of a martial arts movie. She back-flipped while still airborne, barely missing the swipe of another of Bobo's endless supply of arms. This one was like a medieval weapon—a spiked metal ball affixed to a long, rusted chain.

"Seriously? What was *that* when Bobo was still a toy?" she called from midair.

"Plastic chainlink," Piper replied glumly. "Also once cute."

The chain swung back toward Phoebe, and she leaped and ducked again, kicking one leg out forcefully and making contact with the spiked ball. "Ow," she said, grabbing onto her foot while still airborne. "And new shoes!"

"Our wardrobes are seriously taking a beating here, Bobo," Paige said, annoyed. "Not cool."

"Those googly eyes are creepy when they're actually looking at you," Leo observed. "They just roll back and forth in their sockets."

Bobo continued to advance, his various tentacles snapping in every direction. Piper could barely manage to keep him at bay with rapid-fire explosions, none of which seemed to do any permanent damage.

"He wobbles but he doesn't fall down!" she shouted, feeling helpless. "What now?"

"Heads up!" Paige cried. "He's going after the Book of Shadows!" she called out, orbing the precious tome into her hands and out of harm's way.

"And now he's going"—Piper watched as Bobo made his way out of the attic and down into the house—"somewhere else."

Phoebe raced down the stairs after Bobo, while Paige chose the quicker method of orbing. Watching his charges head off, Leo shot his wife a questioning glance.

"No way," she said, shaking her head resolutely. "We can do this without you. Besides," she added, "someone needs to stay with Wyatt. And I don't know how much help you can be if your orbing is still on the fritz."

"I don't like it, but there isn't a lot of time to argue," Leo decided. "You go. Call if you need me, or if one of you is hurt."

Piper flinched as she heard the sound of

breaking glass, followed by a distinctly feminine grunt. "Will do," she promised, rushing down the stairs after her sisters.

She found Phoebe and Bobo in the dining room, Phoebe levitating forward and backward to avoid the swipes of his deadly tentacles. "*What* is Wyatt doing with a toy that has a knife attachment?" she shouted, seeing Piper come down the staircase.

"Well, normally, they're safety scissors," Piper countered. "Very good for motor-skill development. Where's Paige?"

"She's"—Phoebe paused, huffed, and tumbled forward through Bobo's bottom legs—"in the kitchen. Says there's"—she lurched toward one side, then righted herself—"a potion in there that should work."

"We have a potion that vanquishes strange six-legged toys that have come to life?" Piper said dubiously. "Duck, Sis," she said, almost absently, reaching out and exploding the pincher claw as it edged dangerously close to Phoebe's ear. Bobo retracted his claw in anger, then began to creep forward again.

"What I used," Paige said, entering the room behind Piper, "are the extra ingredients we had left over from the cleansing potion we never used. I'm thinking that there's enough overlap in those ingredients and the ingredients you'd use to conquer your childhood demons that we'll be able to say bye-bye to Bobo. I mean, we *are* the Power of Three, after all."

"It's worth a try," Piper agreed, impressed with Paige's reasoning. "And, yeah, if we act together, we should be more powerful."

"Teamwork," Phoebe said, coming to a graceful landing on the floor in between her sisters. Her forehead glistened with sweat. "That's what I like to hear." She grabbed Piper and Paige by the hand so that the three of them were linked together.

Bobo growled at them.

Phoebe squeezed her sisters' hands tighter and improvised:

> *"Childhood memories,*
> *sour or sweet.*
> *We hereby command thee*
> *to retreat!"*

As Phoebe hit the final note of her impromptu spell, Paige stepped forward and hurled the vial of potion at Bobo. It shattered at his feet, enveloping the room in a viscous cloud of smoke.

The sisters dropped hands as they coughed up the heavy air. They waved their arms about, looking to see if Bobo still stood on the opposite side of the curtain of smoke.

"Oh," Paige said, dejected. "He's still—"

Bobo vanished before her eyes.

". . . there?" she finished lamely, confused.

"Did we get him?" Phoebe asked.

"No, uh, I think he actually disappeared," Piper said.

Before the sisters had a chance to investigate, however, the house unleashed itself upon them once again.

"Okay, so, is it just me," Paige asked, "or are those pictures, um, *changing*?"

Indeed, the sepia-toned pictures that normally lined the dining room walls were shifting, giving way to terrifying imagery that the sisters knew was in no way part of their heritage.

"It's not just you," Piper assured her. "Unfortunately."

Just then, the shards of glass from the demolished frames flew in every direction.

"That broke the skin!" Phoebe cried, raising up her arm in self-defense.

"Attic?" Piper asked, shouting to be heard above the chaos.

Paige and Phoebe were already on their way.

"We have good news and bad news," Piper said, leading the cavalry into the attic where Leo stood, gently rocking Wyatt and looking expectant.

"Is Bobo gone?" Leo asked hopefully.

"Well . . ." Piper hedged, taking Wyatt from his father and cradling him against her.

"Yes and no," Paige said breathlessly. "He's gone, but we don't think it has anything to do with us. We tried a potion and a spell, but we're pretty sure he just . . . disappeared, without any help from us."

"Meaning he could just reappear at any time?" Leo looked around the room warily, as if he half expected the demon to burst from the woodwork at any moment. Bobo certainly had the attachments for any kind of entrance he fancied, after all.

"Exactly," Piper confirmed grimly.

"So, what's the good news?" Leo asked.

"The good news is, I think we've got it," Phoebe said, sounding more optimistic than any of them had felt in days. "Our monster, that is. You should thank your wife; she's the one who pieced it all together."

"I can't take all the credit," Piper protested. "Phoebe was the one who made the connection about our being haunted by our childhood memories and fears."

"So, what are you saying?" Leo asked.

"Think about it," Piper said. "All of this weird stuff started happening with the house the same day that Wyatt conjured up the puppy from his drinking cup. We just assumed that it was a one-off mishap. But, in thinking about it, I realized that Bobo was on Wyatt's high-chair tray at the time too!"

"So you think that when Wyatt conjured the puppy, he somehow demonized Bobo at the same time?" Leo asked, putting the pieces together.

Piper nodded. "Exactly. And the demon has been invisible this whole time. I think we have Bobo to thank for our hot-water crisis, the flood in the basement, the black hole in the bathroom, the portal in Paige's bedroom . . ."

"My ability to communicate with the food in our kitchen, and your labor pains," Phoebe finished, managing to look both satisfied and appalled at the same time. She jerked her head toward where the toy Bobo lay lifelessly on the floor. "That kiddie toy has been attacking us in a vulnerable spot—our childhoods! Bobo transformed our childhood house into a nightmare. He even made us doubt our devotion to our home!"

"That must have been why we turned to that page in the Book of Shadows," Paige mused. "The one that made us feel all guilty for turning against our home. Not to mention, our memories," she continued, her tone becoming indignant. "That silly toy totally manipulated me into yearning for a different childhood." She folded her arms across her chest angrily.

"Just give Bobo a goatee and a cigar and we can call him Freud," Piper offered dryly.

"It's a sound theory," Leo confirmed. "So, have you given any thought as to how to vanquish him? Especially considering that he's now invisible."

"I think we're just going to have to shrink ourselves," Paige said.

"I'm not sure how being smaller will really help you," Leo replied, confused.

Phoebe shook her head. "No, not literally. I mean, like, head shrinking. You know—we've just got to get over the childhood trauma that's been manifesting itself in our house."

"But who has time for analysis these days?" Piper cracked.

Phoebe mock glared at her. "Work with me, Sis," she said. "I've got a feeling that we can each deal with our past if we apply ourselves. I have an idea for a crash course in Charmed psychology."

Chapter 10

"First things first," Phoebe muttered to herself, making her way down to the kitchen with cautious determination. "Piper may be the chef in the family, but there's no way I'm going to let myself be scared off by my own kitchen. Empathy is one thing, but this is ridiculous."

She took a deep breath and crossed the threshold into the kitchen, willfully ignoring the shrieks and moans of various foods "killed" and prepared there throughout the ages.

Traditionally, she knew, the hearth had been the center of the home, and the place that families gathered to feel connected to one another. Many of her own childhood memories revolved around pleasant meals with her family. Like Piper, she also recalled Grams' special oatmeal cookies, as well as the soup Grams would make whenever one of the sisters was sick.

When Grams cooked for me, Phoebe thought, *I felt loved. Cared for. Connected.*

She was going to re-create that feeling of connection herself, today. In the Manor kitchen. Memories of Sunday eggs gone sour, or no. She didn't have her own special recipe for any kind of sweet. But she was pretty certain she could wing it.

If you want to make an omelet, you're going to have to break some eggs, she reminded herself. The food that was "sacrificed" here in the Halliwell kitchen was given up for a good cause: to nurture the family and to foster togetherness. How could she feel sorry about that?

We've been turned against our house, so we need to embrace our memories, she decided. *And embrace our home. Starting with the hearth.*

Humming quietly to herself, Phoebe began pulling ingredients out of the refrigerator and dishes and utensils from the overhead cabinets. She noticed that, miraculously, the muffled "food" sounds began to subside as she set to work. The cooking itself was soothing. She hummed to herself as she lovingly prepared a meal for her family—which was exactly what a kitchen was meant for.

For her part, Piper knew that she'd have to work to let the joyful memories of Wyatt's birth overshadow the pain of labor. Easier said than done, to be sure, but certainly not impossible.

While Phoebe and Paige put their own plans into motion, Piper and Leo took Wyatt down to the dining room. As Piper approached the doorway, she felt the first twinges of labor. The contractions radiated from her back to her abdomen, but she gritted her teeth, determined to ignore them. Leo patted her shoulder reassuringly.

"This will work," he promised her. "It has to."

"At this point, I'll try anything," Piper acknowledged. "And—*ow*."

Piper settled herself in one of the dining room chairs as best she could—oddly, she had to remind herself that, although she *felt* pregnant, the reality was that there was no oversized belly to interfere with her sitting down—steeling herself against the waves of pain that washed across her stomach. She smoothed Wyatt's hair off his face.

"I'm going to tell you about the day you were born," she began softly.

Wyatt gazed up at her as though he understood, though, of course, that was fairly unlikely.

"Mommy was very surprised when she realized that you were coming," Piper continued. "And she was a little bit scared, too. But Auntie Phoebe and Auntie Paige were here to help her, and they were very excited to meet you."

"Believe it or not," she went on, warming to what had always been her favorite part of the story of Wyatt's birth, "Auntie Phoebe was the person who delivered you. Which was also a little bit scary, but way better than being in a hospital." She smiled to herself, remembering the pride Phoebe had taken in her role in Wyatt's birth.

Piper sighed and closed her eyes for a moment, basking in the truth of her last statement. Giving birth *had* been painful and terrifying. But the fact that she had delivered Wyatt right in her own home, surrounded by her sisters' love, made the event that much more meaningful, that much more profound.

There was no reason at all, she realized, to be tormented by those memories. The memories of becoming a mother.

"As you're going to learn," she went on, "our family is made up of almost all women. So we expected you to be a girl too. We were very surprised when we realized that we were wrong! But it was the good kind of surprised," she finished, kissing him on the top of his smooth little head, "and we wouldn't trade you for anything in the world."

She sat back in her seat, snuggling Wyatt against her chest. She really did cherish the story of his birth, she realized. Labor pains or no, it had all been well worth it.

From over her shoulder, Leo nudged her gently. She looked up to see him gazing at his wife and son lovingly.

"How are you feeling?" he asked quietly.

Piper paused for a moment, assessing. Her abdomen was still, and she felt better—more relaxed, more free of discomfort—than she had in a good, long time.

She smiled up at her husband. "I feel wonderful," she answered. "I really do."

It was the truth.

Once Piper had conquered her own housey demons, Leo left her with Wyatt to spend some time alone in the place where he was born. The Whitelighter had to get to the bottom of his own orbing problems if he was going to be able to fulfill his duties of watching over the girls—today, and going forward.

He wandered into the living room and sat quietly on the couch. He closed his eyes and took deep, even breaths. His goal was to focus his mental energy on all of the charges he'd looked after for so many years.

The memories were bittersweet; most he had been able to help, some he had not succeeded in saving. It pained him to think of those Innocents and witches that he had lost during his time as a Whitelighter. There were so many, though, for whom he'd been responsible—he couldn't possibly have saved them all.

There were so many. The idea settled over Leo like a thick, heavy blanket. Now that he had stopped to *really* focus, there was no denying that all his life, the welfare of others had been his responsibility. And what a responsibility it was!

As a child, he'd had to care for his many

brothers and sisters. His parents had worked
long hours, and it was often up to Leo to cook
for his siblings, to see that they did their home-
work and went to bed on time, and to mediate
their many disputes, however slight or severe
they may have been.

Then, in his early adulthood, Leo had served
as a wartime medic. Again, there were always
patients to be helped—more patients than any
one person could have possibly rescued, and
Leo had continually felt torn between several
urgent situations at a time.

Eventually, Leo had died and been made a
Whitelighter. He knew that this was truly an
honor, a recognition of the commitment he'd
shown toward caring for others when he was mortal. But being a Whitelighter was both physically
and emotionally exhausting. His work was never
done. Protecting the Charmed Ones was a full-
time job—and it wasn't his only responsibility. He
was constantly juggling his charges, in addition to
trying to find time to be a husband and father.

No wonder I can't seem to orb in one piece, he
realized. *I'm always pulled in a thousand different
directions. I guess I've been stressed about feeling like
I can't ever give my all to any one situation.*

It was hard to admit, but he knew it was the
truth. He loved Piper and Wyatt more than anything, but he couldn't always prioritize his family the way that he would have liked. He
couldn't always be around for Piper when she

needed him. He knew that she understood, and that she supported him, but that didn't necessarily make the sacrifices of his job any easier to deal with.

But that's the way it is, Leo thought to himself. *There isn't an easier solution.* Saving Innocents was his destiny—just as being a husband to Piper and a father to Wyatt were his destiny too. And as long as he honestly gave everyone in his life as much of his passion and energy that he could possibly spare, he was doing his job, and they would appreciate that.

Is it really as simple as that? Leo wondered. *Just reconciling the trouble I have juggling my commitments to so many different people and situations?*

There was only one way to find out.

He closed his eyes in concentration, then focused his energy on orbing off the sofa and into his bedroom upstairs.

When he opened his eyes, he was in the bedroom that he and Piper shared. He nervously walked toward the full-length mirror that stood in one corner, somewhat dreading what he might find.

He needn't have worried. The image that smiled back at him was his own, standing tall and confident.

In one piece.

For her part, Paige had decided that conquering the images she'd been seeing in her bedroom was little more than an issue of mind over matter.

Of course, even something as simple as that was easier said than done.

The fact was that even though Piper and Phoebe went well out of their way to make Paige feel like their blood sister, she did often worry about living up to Prue's legacy as the third member of the Charmed triumverate. She'd often wondered what life would have been like had she grown up alongside her half sisters as one of them, if her parents, a witch and a Whitelighter, had had the same courage that Piper and Leo had and defied the laws of the Elders in order to marry. That was the reason that room had been able to play so many games with her mind—after all, it had only shown her images that her own brain had conjured up, on more than one occasion.

But the bottom line, Paige reminded herself, her delicate ballet flats making a slight squishing sound as she scaled the stairs to her bedroom, *is that I had a childhood of my own. With parents who loved me, whom I loved. And while I may always wonder what it would have been like to grown up with my sisters, I'll never regret the time I had with my adoptive parents. I'm forever grateful to them for taking me in, and showing me so much love.*

She paused in front of her door, wondering for what felt like the billionth time what she'd find behind it. She took a deep breath and shook her shoulder-length hair back from her face.

Desperately wishing that she could cover her eyes with her hand, she reached out and pushed the door open.

What she saw was at once a disappointment and a relief.

Grams and the Charmed sisters were gone. The room glowed. It was still a portal, but this time, she saw her mother and father—her *real* mother and father, the people who adopted her—serving a young Paige her dinner on what could have been any weekday night.

"Can I have ice cream?" Young Paige asked, her voice plaintive.

"Maybe, if you're good, and you eat all of your broccoli, you can have ice cream for dessert," her father suggested, winking at her.

"I want it now," Young Paige insisted, crossing her arms over her chest stubbornly and pouting.

I really was such a terror, Real Paige marveled. *Even when I was, what—eight? Yikes. That was only the beginning.*

She smiled. Even as a terror, her parents had loved her. She'd had a wonderful life with them—even without magic, or her Charmed half sisters.

As Paige smiled to herself, the portal dissolved inward, leaving the room as it usually looked. Her mouth opened in surprise, then relaxed into an easy grin.

"See, Bobo? As far as shrinks go, you could

use some practice," she quipped. She took one last, appraising glance at the bedroom to be sure that the new—real—tableau wouldn't dissolve, and when it remained firmly in place, she closed the door and stepped tentatively into the hall.

"Hello?" she called out. "Is anybody out there? Did anyone else manage to conquer his or her personal demons? Because I think I've finally dealt with my childhood trauma."

By way of answer, Leo materialized in front of her in a shower of glittering orbs. He smiled and waggled his totally intact fingers by way of demonstration. "I can orb again!"

She gave him a quick high five. "We're two for two!" she said, grinning. "And Piper?"

Leo cocked his head to one side, listening for his wife. "She's not in pain anymore," he said. "My guess is that facing her fears in the living room and telling Wyatt the story of his birth trumped the force that was causing the 'labor' pains."

"Nice," Paige said, her smile spreading even wider. "And as for Phoebe"—She stopped, sniffing quizzically. "Do I smell roast chicken?"

"That has to be Phoebe," Leo commented. "And it has to mean that she's gotten over her conversations with food."

"By preparing us a meal?" Paige asked, sincerely surprised. She shrugged. "Well, that makes as much sense as any of this." She patted her stomach. "And, come to think of it, I'm starving!"

• • •

As they tiptoed down the hall, Paige and Leo bumped into Piper, who was all smiles.

"Everything better in your bedroom?" Piper asked.

Paige nodded. "The only memories left are of what actually happened to me," she exclaimed. "Not that the other images weren't interesting to see, but I'm kind of partial to reality."

"I don't blame you," Piper said.

"And you?" Paige bobbed her head in the direction of Piper's stomach.

"You know, I took Wyatt into the dining room and told him the story of how he was born," Piper said. "It's not exactly witchcraft, but it worked like a charm. No pun intended."

"Of course not," Paige replied, rolling her eyes and smiling. "As long as everything's fixed. So, where's Wyatt now?"

"Oh, I orbed him up into his crib for a nap," Leo said, mock casually.

"Well, I guess that means your orbing is back in form," Piper commented.

"Could it possibly be that we've beaten Bobo at his own game?" Paige wondered.

"Don't speak too soon," Piper warned her sister. "We still need to see how things went with Phoebe. Although"—she took a deep breath, sniffing like a bloodhound, and then exhaled slowly, with satisfaction—"judging from the aromas coming from the kitchen, I'd say she has faced her fear. And then seasoned it, diced it, and sautéed it to a crisp. Maybe she and I have more in common than I realized."

"Mmm, you're making me hungry," Paige said, patting her stomach in anticipation.

The door to the kitchen swung open, and a fresh-faced Phoebe beamed at them.

"Did somebody say the magic word?" she asked, waving a wooden spoon at Paige. "Because I've prepared enough food for an army."

"Well, do three witches and a Whitelighter count as an army?" Piper asked.

Phoebe smiled. "Definitely." She waved them in. "I thought it would be more special if we ate in the dining room. This being a special, vanquishing-evil sort of evening, after all."

"Especially since I can go in there now without fear!" Piper chimed in cheerfully.

"I've set the table," Phoebe said, "and I was just carrying in all of the food. Grab a dish!" She waved them in the direction of the kitchen countertops, which were laden with food.

The sisters and Leo happily obliged, stomachs rumbling. They were impressed to discover that Phoebe had prepared a heaping green salad, a thick, creamy potato-leek soup, a roasted chicken, and even some wild rice.

"Jeez, what's for dessert?" Piper cracked, following everyone into the dining room with a pitcher of ice water in hand. She was only half joking.

"Chocolate soufflé," Phoebe tossed back lightly.

"You're kidding," Paige marveled. "It almost makes me wish we were under demon attack more often. I said *almost*," she amended hastily, seeing the looks from her family.

"And . . . *voila*!" Phoebe said, placing the platter of chicken on the table.

"Phoebes, this is incredible," Piper murmured, stopping for a moment to take stock of the room. Phoebe had set the table using the family's best linen and silver, and lit dozens of tiny votive candles in a cluster as a centerpiece. The room was bathed in a soft glow.

"Aw, it was nothing," Phoebe said, waving off Piper's praise. "I just figured, you know, if we were going to reconnect with the house and everything, why not do it in style?"

"Well, if it was style you were after, you've definitely succeeded," Leo said, ruffling his hair with his hands and taking the scene in.

"Yeah, yeah, it's totally gorgeous," Paige said, setting the salad down on the table. She slapped her palms eagerly against the table. "Now—can we eat?"

"One last touch," Phoebe said, rushing back into the kitchen. When she returned, she was brandishing a bottle of champagne. "I found this when I was unpacking the boxes from the kitchen and figured, you know, it's a special occasion. There's some sparkling cider for you,

Paige," she said, in deference to the fact that her half sister didn't drink.

"Awesome," Paige said. " As long as it bubbles, it's the perfect finish."

"I'm so glad you guys like it," Phoebe said. "It was a little dicey when I started on the chicken, but by the time I got to the salad, there were no voices coming at me anymore."

"As it should be," Piper said, patting Phoebe on the back reassuringly. "Food's not supposed to talk unless it's saying, 'Snap, crackle, pop!'"

"Okay, okay," Phoebe said, finally starting to feel a bit embarrassed by all the attention. "Less talking, more eating." She pulled out her chair and readied herself to sit down.

Which was when the table opened up and swallowed their dinner whole.

As the table yawned open, the sisters recoiled. It was as though the entire event were occurring in slow motion. The table groaned, then cracked, splitting along the seams of the wood. Almost soundlessly, the dishes dissolved into the pit, one by one.

"Uh, is it supposed to be doing that?" Paige asked nervously.

"Doubtful," Piper said, rushing in vain to try to freeze the table and save at least some of their china.

"This is not the behavior of a happy house!" Phoebe fretted. "Here I thought the food had gone quiet. Turns out, it was just giving me the silent treatment!"

"Bobo must not be vanquished, then," Leo said logically, watching with horror as the food slid down into the chasm that had opened in the center of the table. "He must've just slipped off into invisibility again."

"Stupid demons and their stupid magical powers," Phoebe said, mourning her lovingly prepared meal. "I was really looking forward to that chicken!"

"Piper, can't you do something?" Paige asked helplessly.

"Like what?" Piper asked. "I don't want to blow up the table. And what good would freezing it do? I mean, we'd save the meal, but that doesn't get us very far with our vanquish, does it? I think I missed my moment, anyway."

"Good point," Paige said. "Darn it." She sighed. "You had to use the good china?" she asked Phoebe.

Phoebe looked contrite. "But it was a celebration," she said.

As the last of the dishes slid down into the bottomless pit, the table seemed to resound with satisfaction. As quickly as it had split apart, the wood began to knit itself together along the grain until the table was good as new.

Only now it was bare.

"You'd never know I just spent the entire evening cooking dinner," Phoebe said sadly.

"And also? That was my favorite tablecloth," Piper added, looking dismayed.

"We all appreciated your gourmet feast," Paige said, tossing a sympathetic arm around Phoebe's shoulder. "Actually, there's one bright side here."

"What's that?" Phoebe asked, her eyes round.

Paige smiled. "Bobo didn't get the soufflé."

"True, Sis," Phoebe said, managing a weak grin of her own. "It's still in the kitchen—barring an unforeseen demon visit. Not that I want to jinx us or anything. I love that you can always see the glass as half full."

"What can I say? I'm an optimist," Paige replied, the concern in her eyes belying the perkiness of her voice.

"Well, I just hope that you're optimistic about our chances against Bobo," Piper said, realizing as she spoke how ridiculous she sounded. "Bobo," she sniffed. "That's about the least ominous name I've ever heard of for a demon."

"Ominous or not, he obviously means business," Leo said. "Which means that we're going to have to take him seriously."

The girls solemnly nodded at one another.

"Well, it may be a small thing, but at least we now know what *doesn't* work against this guy," Piper pointed out.

"Yeah, we can rule a few tactics out," Phoebe agreed. "But I guess we're going to have to widen our research." She placed her hands on her hips and looked pointedly at her sisters. "Attic?"

Piper and Paige nodded in unison. "Attic," they replied.

The three girls and Leo turned and, sighing heavily, made their way upstairs yet again.

Phoebe paused halfway up the staircase and glanced back over her shoulder. "Leo, do you mind making a quick run to the kitchen?" she asked.

He shrugged. "Sure, why?"

Phoebe flushed. "Well, I mean, as long as Bobo didn't get at it, I figure . . . we may as well eat the soufflé."

And at that, at least, everyone had to laugh. They certainly couldn't argue.

Chapter 11

"Here's the thing," Phoebe said, leaning over the Book of Shadows, with deep intent in her eyes. Her plastic-rimmed glasses perched at the tip of her nose as she scanned each page hungrily. "We can't vanquish what we can't see. I mean, we learned that the hard way, right?"

Piper nodded. "Boy, yeah. Lesson learned."

"So what we need," Paige said, coming up behind Phoebe to peer over her shoulder at the Book, "is an anti-invisibility spell."

At that, the book ruffled quietly, until it spilled open to a particular page.

"Ask, and ye shall receive," Leo quipped.

Phoebe pushed her glasses back up on her nose and leaned forward. She cleared her throat dramatically, preparing to read the spell aloud.

"Demon of night,
demon of day.
Demon of air,

> *show us the way.*
> *Allow your image*
> *to hereby appear.*
> *We witches shall vanquish.*
> *It matters not where."*

She put her hands on her hips and gazed at her sisters and brother-in-law. "What do you think?"

"It's a good start," Piper said, gnawing on a fingernail.

Phoebe cocked her head to one side questioningly. She could read Piper's tone of voice all too well. "But?" she said.

Piper shrugged sheepishly. "But maybe it's not . . . enough? I mean, we've used spells against him, and we've used potions."

"We've totally unleashed the Power of Three on him," Paige reminded everyone. "It didn't seem to do us much good."

"Come on, people," Phoebe said, clapping her hands together in a burst of energy. "What happened to the glass being half full?"

"It ran out," Paige said glumly, thrusting out her lower lip in a pout. She collapsed on the window seat in the corner, resting her chin in her hands.

Phoebe shook her head determinedly. "Nope, nuh-uh. Not good enough. We're the Charmed Ones. There's no way that this armchair psychologist is going to get the best of us."

"He's not even a psychologist," Paige protested, arching one perfect eyebrow. "He's a toy."

"Yeah, and this has all been child's play—*not*," Piper chimed in, obviously feeling somewhat defeated as well.

"We've got a spell," Phoebe said. "It's stronger than the one that we made up before. After all, it doesn't just come from us. It has the power of our ancestors behind it—the ones who came before us in this house, that is. Maybe I can tweak it a little bit, add some language to make it our own."

Piper nodded, looking the slightest bit encouraged for the first time since the girls had ventured back into the attic. "That could work."

Paige ran her fingers through her hair, deep in thought. "Mercury!" she exclaimed finally, her hazel eyes sparkling with renewed vigor.

"Mercury what?" Piper asked, slightly suspicious.

"Mercury could be what was missing from the last potion," Paige offered. "I mean, based on the ingredients we put together, it *should* have vanquished Bobo. But it didn't."

"Clearly not," Piper said dryly.

"With a dash of mercury, the potion should work more swiftly," Paige said, thinking aloud. "We'll say the spell, toss the potion, and *whammo*—Bobo will be gone in the blink of an eye!"

"I still think we're missing something," Piper said.

"Don't be so negative," Phoebe admonished, wagging a finger at her sister.

Leo frowned from his perch in the corner of the room. "She's right, though. There has to be something else. Some other step. If it were that easy to vanquish Bobo, you would have done it by now."

"Huh," Paige said, looking thoughtful. "I think we can do with a little less support from the peanut gallery." At Leo's crushed expression, she rushed to correct herself. "No, you're right," she said. "I'm just frustrated." She drummed her fingers on the windowsill.

"Okay, you guys," Phoebe said, perking up from behind the stand where the Book of Shadows rested. "Tell me if I'm crazy."

"You're crazy," Piper put in.

"*After* you hear me out," Phoebe insisted with mock indignation. "Listen. When the Woogie manifested himself to me in the house, where was it?"

"That was before my time," Paige replied, "but I've heard the story. The basement."

"And when Cole briefly managed to take control of the Manor," she asked, wincing at the mention of her ex-husband and the one-time Source of All Evil, "where was the axis of his black magic here?"

"The basement," Piper nodded, catching on.

"So I think it's safe to say that evil, when it does show its face here—"

"Which is more often than I'd like," Piper cut in.

"It's safe to say that, when evil drops in, it originates from a hotspot in the basement," Phoebe speculated. "And when it's not that strong, we can vanquish it no matter where it is in the house. Especially since we've got the Power of Three."

"I'm sensing a 'but' somewhere in this theory," Paige chimed in.

Phoebe nodded, warming to her idea. "Exactly. *But*," she went on, dramatically, "Bobo is a representation of *our* deepest psychological fears. So we've got to get him down to the basement—where his vibe is strongest—in order to do away with him."

Piper looked pensive for a moment. Then she spoke. "Yeah, okay, I hear what you're saying," she said. "But won't bringing him to the basement make him stronger?"

"Normally, I'd say yes," Phoebe replied. "But in this case, he's got us at our cores. Therefore, I think the only way to truly strike back and vanquish him once and for all is to get *him* at *his* core."

"So, basement," Paige said, looking as though she could see the logic in Phoebe's plan. Which, actually, she could.

"I'd say you were nuts," Piper remarked slowly, "but since none of us have been able to come up with a better idea . . ."

Phoebe clapped her hands together gleefully. "I knew you'd go for this plan!"

"You can modify the spell?" Piper asked.

Phoebe nodded dutifully.

"And I can whip up a new potion," Paige said.

"Good thinking," Leo said, patting Piper on the back. "I say we get to all of this stuff first thing tomorrow."

"Tomorrow?" Piper asked, incredulous.

Leo nodded. "Look," he said, swallowing hard. "Vanquishing Bobo is obviously going to take all of your strength. You should get a good night's sleep."

"Fine," Piper grumbled, capitulating. "But first I want another helping of the soufflé."

"That?" Phoebe asked, eyes twinkling mischieviously. "That part's easy."

The next morning, the sisters arose bright and early to put their plan into action. They intended to conjure Bobo—this time in the basement, of course—before saying the new and improved spell and giving him a healthy dose of Paige's potion (now with mercury!). Preparations had begun at dawn, with Phoebe familiarizing her sisters with the new wording of the spell, and Paige's potion bubbling away on the kitchen range. Leo had fed Wyatt and placed him in his playpen for the morning, so that he could dedicate himself to the Charmed Ones should they need him. From the Halliwell sisters' point of view, this morning was all Bobo, all the time.

Which was why they were sort of surprised when the doorbell rang promptly at ten a.m.

"Whatever they're selling, we don't want any," Piper yelled from the kitchen. She was helping Paige oversee the potion mixing, and the two had left it to either Phoebe or Leo to answer the door.

"Uh, nothing for sale," Phoebe called back uncertainly. "Piper, you might want to come out here!"

"Oh, for Pete's sake," Piper groused, wiping her hands on a dishrag and making her way to the front hallway. "Who is it, anyw—oh!" she said, stopping short.

"We brought the graham crackers," Celeste— she of Mommy and Me, that was—chirped brightly, her voice laden with its signature cheer.

"You brought . . . but . . . *why* did you bring graham crackers?" Piper asked, thoroughly confused.

"She brought them for snack time. For Mommy and Me," Phoebe said, her eyes boring holes into her sister's face. "Today is your turn to hostess."

Piper forced the corners of her mouth upward into a smile. "Right!" she said, clapping her hands together enthusiastically, hoping that the glint of desperation in her eyes didn't give her away.

"Holly called you," Celeste said. "After the last time, at my house, Holly was planning to host, but she has a nasty cold. You said you could do it 'whenever.'"

"That . . . I did?" Piper said with slowly dawning horror. "That I did." She took a deep breath, taking in the long line of women—with toddlers in tow—standing behind Celeste. They came bearing snacks, formula, toys, and good will. At *exactly* the worst possible time.

Did I really say, "whenever"? Piper thought, dizzy. *Yeah, I guess I did.*

"Piper?" Phoebe asked, her voiced tinged with saccharine, "can I see you inside for just an *eensy* moment?" She grabbed her sister by the wrist and dragged her into the living room and out of earshot.

Once they were safely inside, she shook Piper, her eyes flashing wildly. "Piper, I love you, but you cannot seriously be considering letting those moms into our house on demon-cleaning day!" she protested, her voice rising to a squeak.

"Yeah, I hear you, Sis, but what would you have me do? I mean, Celeste is right—I *did* offer for them to come by *anytime.* Apparently, I invited them to come by *this* time."

"Can't you un-offer?" Phoebe asked insistently.

Piper sighed. "In a perfect world, sure. But this is hardly a perfect world. This is a world where we're tormented by children's toys and our own childhood memories. Which is exactly what you want when your Mommy and Me group comes to call." Now Piper looked panicked. "Oh, God. What am I going to do? I can't send them away. They already think I'm a flake, I've missed so many meetings for other witchy business. Ugh. *Why* did I ever think I could have any semblance of a normal life, with normal friends?"

Seeing her sister on the verge of losing it, Phoebe softened a little. "Breathe. We'll deal. Look, take them up to the attic. That's the safe room."

Piper nodded, color slowly returning to her cheeks. "The attic. Good call."

"Just give me a minute to clear away the Book of Shadows and anything else that could raise any eyebrows," Phoebe suggested. "I'll get Leo to help. We can make it look like an awesome playroom, I'm sure."

"Perfect, Phoebes," Piper said, relief flooding across her pretty features. "You're a lifesaver."

Phoebe grinned. "Yeah, I know," she said happily. "But that's what baby sisters are for."

Half an hour—and several packets of graham crackers—later, the Mommy and Me group was firmly ensconced in the attic and Piper, Paige, and Phoebe were ready to put their plan to vanquish Bobo into action.

"Do you think they suspected anything?" Piper asked, as she and her sisters made their way down the stairs into the dark and foreboding basement.

"Well, they were definitely curious about my scrying crystals," Paige admitted, "but I think I threw them off the scent when I explained that the crystals were New Age earrings."

"Yeah, quick thinking," Piper said gratefully.

"Anyway, that's not the point," Paige went on. "Leo is up there playing happy homemaker with the mommies. So the point is to get Bobo to show himself and to vanquish him, once and for all."

"You bet," Phoebe stage-whispered, as though she were afraid that Bobo was lurking somewhere, still invisible, and eavesdropping on them at that very moment.

"Does everyone have a vial of potion?" Paige asked.

Phoebe and Piper called out in the affirmative.

Reaching the basement floor, Piper flicked on a light. The room was bathed in a low, slightly orange light.

"Eh. Still creepy," Piper mused. "Let's hope that when Bobo shows, he'll be equally freaked."

"Not funny," Phoebe said, more to herself than to her sisters. "And, generally speaking, it's hard to scare scary things."

"It's a little bit funny," Piper said. "I mean, all things considered."

"Sure, ha, ha, whatever," Phoebe retorted, digging into the front pocket of her jeans in

search of her specially reworded spell. "Okay."
She turned to her sisters. "You think we should
hold hands?"

Paige shrugged. "It can only make us
stronger."

"Good call," Phoebe said, nodding. She
looped a pinky through Paige's slender fingers,
still clutching her new spell.

The girls closed their eyes and recited in unison:

> *"Demon of night,*
> *demon of day.*
> *Demon of ours,*
> *show us the w—"*

The door to the basement burst open and the
room was flooded with light.

"Piper?" a sharp voice trilled.

"Uh, Celeste?" Piper asked, her voice thick
with uncertainty.

"*There* you are!" Celeste said, starting down
the basement stairs.

"Oh, Celeste—no," Piper protested, rushing
up the staircase to cut her friend off at the pass.
"You don't have to come down here. My sisters
and I thought . . . um, we thought we smelled . . ."

"A gas leak!" Paige chimed in brightly.

"Exactly, a gas leak," Piper finished weakly.
"You know, because of that work I mentioned
we were having done . . ."

Celeste sniffed at the air cautiously. "Hmm. I

suppose you could be right. There is a certain . . . odor down here."

Piper ignored that comment. "Can I . . . help you with anything?" she asked, widening her eyes and willing herself to be patient. After all, Celeste had no idea •that the sisters were in prime vanquishing mode!

"Well, I was just looking for some milk," Celeste said, "and I didn't know if you had set any cartons aside especially for Mommy and Me."

From behind her, Nancy, another eager mommy, appeared in the basement doorway.

"Piper? Did Celeste talk to you about the milk?" she asked. "Also, some of the kids are fussing. They're probably hungry. Do you have any animal crackers?"

"Oh, ah, you can just help yourself to whatever you find in the refrigerator," Piper said, feeling that the whole scene was growing ever more surreal. "Or, you know, Leo should be able to help you. I know he's technically a daddy, but you'd be surprised at how good he is at these things."

Celeste laughed maniacally, as though this were the funniest thing she'd ever heard in her life. "Of *course*." Her head bobbed up and down earnestly. "But he seems to have disappeared."

"Maybe it was just a bathroom break?" Paige suggested. She was obviously itching to get the Bobo show going as well.

"Yup, that's what it was, I bet!" Piper said enthusiastically, every ounce of psychic energy in her body focused on sending Celeste back upstairs into the safety of the attic. "You just go up there and wait for him! I'll be right up as soon as the whole 'gas leak' thing is sorted out!"

"Well," Celeste hedged, looking doubtful. "Okay."

"Great, perfect, be up in a few," Piper replied, gently escorting Celeste back up the stairs and closing the basement door behind her.

Once the door was shut, she turned back to her sisters. "Close call," she said grimly. "Now, can we get this demon vanquished before I'm officially banned from the neighborhood playgroup?"

"Where were we?" Phoebe asked, latching on to her sisters' hands again. "Ahem:"

> *"Demon of night,*
> *demon of day.*
> *Demon of ours,*
> *show us the way.*
> *Allow your image*
> *to hereby appear.*
> *We witches shall vanquish*
> *our childhood fears."*

The girls paused expectantly.

"Right," Paige said, after a beat. "So, Bobo, that would be your cue."

"Here, Bobo," Phoebe called. She peered cautiously around the room, but it looked like the demon hadn't yet materialized. Whether this was a good thing or not still remained to be seen.

"Maybe he gave up and left on his own?" Piper suggested, knowing as she said it that it was a feeble last-ditch.

Suddenly, from a dark and shadowy corner of the basement, the cement flooring began to ripple.

"I'm thinking, no," Paige quipped, watching as the floor buckled and expanded beneath them.

"Yeah, good call," Piper agreed. "Check that out."

She pointed, and the sisters followed her gaze. Along the wall, the concrete cinderblocks that lined the interior of the basement were slowly loosening and pushing outward into the room, crashing against the floor and smashing into powdery rubble. The one lone window that opened into the basement slid up and down, its wooden frame splintering.

"That's new," Piper commented.

"That's not!" Paige called out, eyes widening.

From behind the wall, Bobo charged. He was tall as ever, and his tentacles swung wildly. Phoebe leaped into the air in a martial arts pose to avoid him, kicking out with her legs as she simultaneously blocked her head with her upper arms.

"Piper, can you freeze him?" she yelled, panting with exertion.

Piper flung her arms at Bobo and shot energy from the tips of her fingers. The magic hit Bobo and slid harmlessly off him as though he were wearing a suit of armor.

"Apparently not," Piper replied helplessly, continuing to try to freeze him in rapid-fire succession, and with the same results (or complete lack thereof) each time. "This guy takes a licking and keeps on ticking!"

"Literally!" Paige shouted, exasperated. "Since he has that stupid wind-up heartbeat inside!"

"Look, I'm sorry!" Piper retorted, getting a little bit cranky. "Wyatt thought it was soothing!"

"Okay, this is not the time to be flipping out on each other," Phoebe reminded her sisters. She was back on the ground, upright, breathing heavily and glistening with a soft sheen of sweat. "Maybe we need to get a little potion action going?"

"It's a thought," Piper said, raising her vial up as her sisters did the same.

They stretched their arms out, ready to throw—

Which was when Bobo reared his head back and roared, then charged forward. In an instant, he flicked one rope-edged tentacle toward them, knocking all of their vials to the floor. The glass shattered on impact, potion seeping across concrete, where it smoked but did no further damage.

"So glad I got up at sunrise to work on that," Paige said sadly, clearly frustrated.

Bobo continued to advance on the girls, his crazed eyes swirling in their sockets and his pincher snapping. The trio edged backward until they stood, huddled, just outside a closet door.

Desperately, Piper flung her hands out again to zap him. She managed to sear off his bladed tentacles, and gave a triumphant whoop. "Now you're going to have to cut it out," she gasped, rolling her eyes at her own pun.

But her moment of victory didn't last long. Just as quickly as the appendage had been amputated, it began to regenerate itself, until the two sharp blades gleamed in what little light made its way into the basement.

"He's invincible?" Piper wondered aloud, breathing heavily.

"That's no good," Paige commented, shaking her head.

As if in response, Bobo bared his fangs—jagged, razor-sharp fangs, at that—and they shrieked in unison.

"Um, which is worse, Bobo—or the Closet Monster?" Paige asked.

"Bobo," Piper replied simply. "Definitely

Bobo." She reached behind her and, hands shaking, pried the closet door open. She and her sisters scurried inside.

And waited, breathless.

Chapter 12

"So," Phoebe began, her voice little more than a whisper. "I'll go first. I'm not afraid to say it. We seem to be—how do I put this—trapped in the closet."

"Yeah, looks that way," Piper agreed. "Not too sure what to do about it."

"Wait, Piper, Phoebe," Paige began, "this is ridiculous. We're the Charmed Ones. We're all-powerful witches. What are we doing hiding out in a closet from an oversized kiddie toy?"

"Avoiding our childhood demons," Phoebe pointed out rather logically. "And reevaluating whether or not we need some industrial-strength therapy."

"Given that . . . that *thing* out there is a manifestation of our, um, collective issues, I'd say that's a resounding 'yes,'" Paige replied. "But there isn't exactly time for that now. And anyway, sometimes a cigar is just a cigar. And, this demon is *just* a demon. It has to be.

There's no way it's stronger than we are!"

"Right," Piper said, sounding somewhat defeated. "In which case, why does it seem to be winning this battle?"

"Because it's not your battle to wage."

The girls gasped as the closet door burst open, tensing for an onslaught from Bobo. But all they saw was Leo, looking wide-awake and fully energized. Wyatt cooed happily in his arms.

"Leo!" Piper said, disbelieving. "Why did you bring our baby down here, to where, I might remind you, my sisters and I are fighting black magic? Why didn't you leave him upstairs with other Mommy and Me's, where it was safe? The basement is strictly off-limits until Bobo is gone for good."

"Because, Piper," Leo began, sounding very excited and very sure of himself. "I figured it out."

"Figured what out?" Phoebe asked.

"The reason that you three haven't been able to vanquish Bobo permanently," Leo continued. "I've got it, finally."

"Enlighten us," Piper said. Her face softened and she added, "Please. 'Cause I gotta tell you, we're at the end of our rope."

"Bobo is Wyatt's toy," Leo reminded the girls. "And, ultimately, Wyatt's the one who conjured him. Bobo's been preying on all of our deepest childhood fears, and in order to conquer those fears, we all had to face them. But if we want Bobo to be gone for good? Well, that's Wyatt's responsibility."

"So you're saying we're just going to unleash that *thing* out there on our son?" Piper asked, shocked.

"Piper, I'm not any happier about it than you are," Leo said. "But I'm pretty sure it's what we need to do."

"It makes sense, Piper," Phoebe said gently, placing a hand on her sister's shoulder. "Really, it does."

"Besides," Paige added, "Wyatt has shown us on more than one occasion that he can totally take care of himself. He's done plenty of demon busting on his own."

"That's true," Piper said grudgingly. "I suppose." She sighed, gazing at her son for a long beat. "Okay," she said finally. "But we're going to be right behind him."

"Every step of the way," Leo echoed.

One by one, the sisters and Leo tiptoed out of the closet. Surprisingly, the basement was still.

"Where'd Bobo go?" Paige asked. "There are only so many places a six-armed, eight-foot-tall demon can hide."

Silently, Leo jerked his head toward the farthest corner of the room. Bobo was crouched there, growling softly, and obviously waiting for his prey to emerge.

Upon laying eyes on Bobo, Wyatt promptly

began to wail as if the Devil himself were upon him.

Which, by Wyatt's standards, is sort of accurate, Piper thought to herself, her maternal instincts surging.

"It's okay, honey," Piper coaxed in her most level and soothing voice. "You're stronger than the big bad demon. He can't hurt you if you just use your powers."

Wyatt managed to take two wobbly steps forward, then sat down with a thud, his gaze never leaving Bobo's menacing tentacles.

As Wyatt plopped to the ground, Bobo's growls grew louder. He reared up again and began to twirl his many arms in the direction of the sisters, Wyatt, and Leo. Wyatt, in turn, shrieked to the high heavens.

"Baby, don't be scared," Phoebe called out. "He's just a silly little toy. Look at how his funny eyes roll around in his head."

Wyatt's sniffles calmed momentarily as he regarded Bobo's giant googly eyes.

"And look at those long, floppy arms," Paige added. "You love to play with those. That's how you fall asleep every night."

Bobo growled and swiped the air with his mace. Fortunately, it passed harmlessly over Wyatt's head.

"Bobo is your friend, Wyatt," Leo said. "When you want him to be."

At that, the final affront, Bobo charged forward

and gnashed his teeth at Piper, who hovered anxiously behind Wyatt. Piper reached out instinctively, planning to toss a small explosion at Bobo. She knew it wouldn't stop him, but it would subdue him momentarily. And that was better than nothing. She flung her hands forward—

Which was when Wyatt opened his mouth, wailed once more, and pointed one chubby finger directly at his one-time playmate come to life.

Poof!

With a gurgly giggle from baby Wyatt, Bobo was gone.

As the smoke from Bobo's vanquish cleared, the sisters and Leo looked at each other questioningly.

"Is that it?" Paige asked, sounding stunned. "It was really that easy?"

Wyatt grinned and clapped his little hands together.

"I guess so," Piper said, fairly shell-shocked herself. She scooped Wyatt up from the ground and smothered him in kisses. "Aren't you just Mommy's little boy, saving the day?" she asked him. "Aren't you Charmed just like your mommy?"

"Not just Charmed," Leo pointed out. "He's obviously really protective of you. Which should go without mentioning."

"Why do you say that?" Piper asked, frankly curious.

"Well, you know," Leo teased, a smile spreading across his handsome face. "It's like Freud said. If it's not one thing, it's your mother."

The girls groaned good-naturedly. As long as the demon was gone, they could all relax.

"I'll let that corny joke go," Piper said, grinning. "But only because I've got somewhere to be. I believe there is a Mommy and Me group waiting up in the attic for the guest of honor?" She planted one more smooch on Wyatt's round cheek for good measure.

"Oh!" Leo said, a look of horror crossing his face. "That reminds me.

"I think I told Celeste I would bring her some milk."

Epilogue

"We're home!" Phoebe trilled, rushing through the front door with Paige hot on her heels. "And wait until you see the shoes we got. Oh—and Paige got the cutest little ruffley shrug, you have to see it on her!"

The girls dashed through the door to the kitchen with their shopping bags in tow, beaming at Piper, who sat at the kitchen table, contentedly sipping a mug of tea.

"Shh," she said quietly. "I just put Wyatt down. And after yesterday's adventures in psychoanalysis, he needs the rest."

"We're sorry," Phoebe said in her best stage whisper. She pulled up a chair and dropped her shopping bags on the floor in a heap. "But, really, it is a very cute sweater."

"I'm going to have to agree with her," Paige said, smiling widely. "Retail therapy is one of my favorite ways to unwind after some serious battling of evil."

"You deserve it," Piper said, smiling back at her hypercharged sisters. "Especially since Bobo wreaked some *serious* havoc on your wardrobes."

"That's exactly what I said," Paige agreed, nodding her head. "So, did you get to do any relaxing of your own while we were out?"

Piper cocked her head to one side. "Well, let's see," she began. "First I took Wyatt for a walk around the block—I figured that after so many days cooped up in the house, we could both use the fresh air."

"Good thinking," Phoebe said approvingly.

"Then I tidied up the house a little bit," Piper continued. "Which I know wouldn't be all that soothing for you guys, but it's sort of necessary for my own sanity. What can I say? I'm wacky that way."

"That's who you are—that's why we love you!" Paige said agreeably. "And anyway, better you than me." She smiled to show that she was only joking.

"Thanks, sweetie," Piper said. "Then Wyatt and I read a story, and now he's sleeping—if you'll pardon the expression—like a baby. And here I am. Enjoying a quiet afternoon cup of tea." She inhaled deeply and exhaled slowly, clearly relishing in her "Piper time." "I have to say, I am completely and totally, 100 percent relaxed."

The sisters paused, taking in the tranquility of the moment.

Crash!

Their collective reverie was broken by the sound of a horrible clanking coming from the direction of the basement.

"Uh, I hate to break it to you, Piper, but that's not a very peaceful noise," Phoebe said, raising an eyebrow.

"Yes, that's why I'm trying to block it out," Piper agreed. "I had some music on before you two got home."

Another loud crashing sound boomed from downstairs, followed by a clattering that echoed off the very baseboards of the house.

"Okay, I'll bite," Paige said, sighing deeply. "*What* is that noise?"

"Well, I'm sure you two can recall that when Bobo manifested yesterday, he took some of the basement walls down with him. Not to mention the scorch marks from where Wyatt blew him away." She smiled fondly at the memory of her son sticking up for his mother so courageously. "And, ah, he also tore up some of the concrete floor. So Leo's down there working on some home repairs."

As Piper finished her explanation, the sisters were amused to overhear Leo let out a colorful string of phrases, followed by yet another sonic boom.

The girls giggled.

"Poor Leo," Phoebe said. "Forget the pressures of being a Whitelighter. A handyman's work is never done."

"Yeah," Piper said fondly. "I guess we're stuck with this fixer-upper."

"You know you wouldn't have it any other way," Paige said, still cracking up.

"So true," Piper replied. "Be it ever so humble—"

She and her sisters finished the thought in unison.

"There's no place like home!"

About the Author

Micol Ostow is a writer and editor of books for children, tweens, and teens. She lives and works (but rarely sleeps) in New York City.

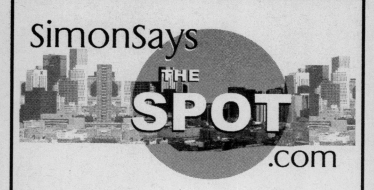